Praise for Janelle Denison

"Kudos to Ms. Denison for her fantastic,
hot, steamy love stories and the heroes that
leave you wishing you had one just like him!"
—*A Romance Review*

"Hotter than hot."
—*All About Romance*

"Fast-paced action, realistic dialogue
and unbelievably sexy situations all blend together
for a definite keeper!"
—*Escape to Romance*

"Denison writes a smart and
snappy contemporary romance novel!"
—*Dreamworld Book Reviews* on *Too Wilde to Tame*

"Hold on tight, this one's a page-turner!"
—*RT Book Reviews* on *Into the Night*

"A superior blend of humor
and simmering sensuality."
—*RT Book Reviews* on *Pure Indulgence*

Dear Reader,

As I was writing *No Strings...* an interesting theme stood out for me: traditional matchmaking vs. modern matchmaking, and how each has its own benefits. Traditional matchmaking is as old as time and there is a lot of intuition involved, while the more modern version seems to focus on charts and questionnaires that give couples a more practical, scientific approach to finding that special someone.

The internet is bursting with all sorts of websites that promise to find someone you're compatible with, but sometimes chemistry is more than just about a checklist of things that two people have in common. Sometimes it's about two people who are slightly opposite, yet manage to work through those differences and learn to compromise.

In *No Strings...* my hero and heroine are sent to a matchmaking resort to work on an ad campaign. Both have been unlucky in love in the past and are cynical when it comes to any kind of matchmaking method. But there's something magical and seductive about this resort that makes them both realize that maybe they really are meant for one another.

I enjoy hearing from readers. You can visit me at www.janelledenison.com, friend me at Facebook at www.facebook.com/janelledenisonfanpage, or chat with me at my blog, www.plotmonkeys.com.

Enjoy!

Janelle Denison

No Strings...

Janelle Denison

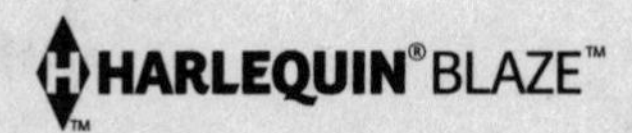

Recycling programs
for this product may
not exist in your area.

ISBN-13: 978-0-373-79758-5

NO STRINGS...

This edition published by arrangement with Harlequin Books S.A.

For questions and comments about the quality of this book, please contact us at CustomerService@Harlequin.com.

Printed in U.S.A.

ABOUT THE AUTHOR

Janelle Denison is a *USA TODAY* bestselling author of more than fifty sensual contemporary romance novels; she has written for Harlequin Blaze, Kensington Brava, Berkley and St. Martin's Press. She is a two-time recipient of a National Reader's Choice award, and has also been nominated for a prestigious RITA® Award. Originally a California native, she now calls Oregon home. She resides in the Portland area with her husband and daughters and can't imagine a more beautiful place to live. When not writing, she can be found exploring the great Northwest, from the gorgeous beaches to the amazing waterfalls and lush mountains.

To learn more about Janelle and her upcoming releases, you can visit her at www.janelledenison.com, friend her at Facebook, www.facebook.com/janelledenisonfanpage, or chat with her at her blog, www.plotmonkeys.com.

To Don.
Thank you for the best twenty-six years of my life!

1

"DON'T LOOK NOW, but Aiden just walked in." That statement was followed up with a long, lingering sigh of adoration.

Waiting in line to order her morning coffee, Chloe Reiss smiled at her coworker Holly, who was standing in front of her, facing the line of people behind them. Her friend had a dreamy, wistful look on her face, one that was common among most of the women who set eyes on Aiden Landry, and especially for the ones who worked with him at Perry & Associates. The man was gorgeous, sexy and charming—a lethal combination any female with a healthy libido was quick to appreciate.

Including Chloe. Because she'd never be able to touch *that,* looking was all she had the luxury of doing. She and Aiden worked for the same ad agency and had been required to sign a strict "no dating coworkers" agreement as part of their employment as advertising executives. She understood the need for such a rule, especially in a career where creativity, drive and focus was key. Dating was a huge distraction, and more times than not, it ended in a messy breakup that made working together difficult and awkward, if not impossible.

But Chloe had to admit that the firm's policy was both a blessing and a curse. A blessing, because it kept her from doing something incredibly foolish—like giving in to the heated attraction between her and Aiden and doing all kinds of wicked things with him. A curse, because it kept her from experiencing what she was certain would be the most phenomenal sex she'd ever had. As it was, a little harmless flirtation would be all that they'd ever indulge in, but there were definitely times she wished she could straddle the line between business and pleasure with Aiden.

She and Holly took a step forward in the line, and Chloe casually glanced over her shoulder. Piercing blue eyes met hers, as if Aiden had been waiting for her to turn around. The slow, purely male smile easing up the corner of his mouth gave her a jolt of instantaneous awareness, stronger than any shot of caffeine ever could. In return, she waggled her fingers at him in a playful morning greeting before returning her attention to Holly.

"Coffee is on me this morning," Chloe said as they stepped up to the barista. The day was off to a fine start.

Holly asked for a Chai tea, and Chloe ordered a skinny vanilla latte for herself and a cappuccino with one packet of sugar for Aiden. Two years of them working together as account executives for Perry & Associates had given her some insight into the man's vices. She knew how he liked his morning java, and because coworkers often met up after hours at the Executive Bar located on the ground floor of the high rise where they worked, she also knew his alcoholic beverage of choice was Glenlivit Scotch neat.

After paying for the drinks, she and Holly picked up their orders at the other end of the counter.

"Thanks for the tea," Holly said, and shifted anxiously on her feet. "I hate to bolt on you, but I have a marketing report that's due on Leland's desk first thing this morning. You know he'll start bellowing if it's not in his chubby little hands at eight o'clock sharp."

Chloe grinned at Holly's apt description of her marketing supervisor. "Go ahead. I'll talk to you later."

Holly took off for the bank of elevators located in the lobby outside of the coffee shop, and Chloe headed toward Aiden, two cups of brew in her hands. Still waiting in line, he watched her approach, a dark, curious brow raised as she neared. The man was model gorgeous, with chiseled features and a sensual mouth. His pitch-black hair, cut into a neat, short style, combined with those devastatingly sapphire blue eyes, was one helluva potent combination that never failed to make her a little breathless when all that hotness was directed at her—as it was right now.

In Chloe's estimation, Aiden was total male perfection, and then some. Tall, lean and built like a Greek God, he wore the expensive cut of his tailored suit with flawless ease and effortless sophistication. The times he took off his jacket, usually by the end of the workday, was always an added visual treat for Chloe, because those crisp white dress shirts he favored showcased his broad shoulders and hinted at the athletically honed body beneath. And when he rolled up the sleeves and exposed those strong forearms...well, she wasn't a girl prone to swooning, but there was just something incredibly arousing about a man with arms and hands that spoke of inherent power and strength that did it for her in a major way.

And Aiden Landry had a pair of big, strong hands, and nice long, capable fingers. The kind she imagined could give a woman all kinds of erotic pleasure. Unfortunately, she'd never find out for real. Instead, she'd just have to be satisfied with the fantasies she spun in her head.

Reaching Aiden, she handed him the tall paper cup of espresso and cream, topped with a generous dollop of foam. "I've got you covered this morning. Cappuccino with one packet of sugar."

"Thanks." He smiled his gratitude as he stepped out of the coffee line and fell into step beside Chloe as they headed for the building's elevators. "Looks like I owe you one."

She cast him a sidelong glance filled with teasing intent. "You know I like to keep it that way."

Amusement glimmered in his eyes. "What? Me, owing you?"

She took a drink of her latte and nodded. "You never know when an outstanding favor might come in handy."

He chuckled, the deep, smooth sound stroking across her senses like an intimate caress. "Yeah, you like having me indebted to you, don't you?"

"Oh, absolutely," she agreed, enjoying their flirtatious banter. It gave her an extra pep in her step, and released all kinds of feel-good endorphins inside her. "You know what they say. Keep your friends close, and your work rival even closer."

The corner of his mouth quirked with a playful grin. "Are you saying you like having me on a short leash?"

"The shorter, the better." They were joking, of course, as they'd done for the past two years. But oh, the images that flooded her mind, of him wearing nothing but a leather studded collar and her tugging on a chrome chain leash like he was her personal plaything, willing to obey her every command, was a heady fantasy, indeed.

They arrived at the elevators, and since it was close to eight o'clock in the morning, there was a mad rush for those who had a time clock to punch. The Boston high rise, located in the financial district, boasted forty-two floors and was comprised of a few hundred companies and firms, which made for a congested elevator ride in the morning and at quitting time. Since she and Aiden weren't in any big hurry, they sipped their coffees and gradually shuffled their way forward.

"Are you ready for your presentation for Organic Kitty this morning?" he asked, referring to the pitches she'd been working on for the past month.

She always had a little flutter of nerves the morning of any client meeting, and this one was no exception, especially since she was going it solo, which was happening more and more lately as she built her own client base. She felt confident about her overall campaign and was certain she'd meet, or exceed, all of the client's expectations.

"I was up until two this morning putting the final touches on the proposal, and I'm pretty damn happy about it," she told him.

"You know I'll be at the meeting." He sipped his cappuccino, his eyes crinkling slightly at the corners as he grinned mischievously. "For moral support, of course."

"Of course," she replied drolly, and rolled her eyes, not buying his "moral support" statement for a minute. And he knew it, too.

Perry & Associates had a lax policy about allowing other employees to sit in on presentations, as a learning experience and to keep abreast of what the agency was doing, so long as there were no disruptions. But for someone as experienced as Aiden, his strategy was more about keeping himself informed on what the competition was doing. Chloe was just as guilty of doing it to his presentations, too.

But while there had been some incidences of back-stabbing with other employees, she and Aiden had never stooped to that level. Over the years, they'd developed a mutual respect for one another and their work, probably because they'd started out on the same marketing team that had required them to work together on various projects. They'd learned early on to trust one another with their ideas and campaigns, but now, with each of them building their own client base, there was a level of competition between them that kept them both striving to one up the other.

And ultimately, they both had their eye on the next rung in the corporate ad agency ladder. Word had gotten out that Perry was looking to promote someone within the firm to a senior executive position within the next few months, and that person would be given their own team to manage. It was a huge coup, and one that Chloe had every intention of achieving. She'd worked extremely hard establishing herself as a qualified leader within the firm, and she'd like to think she deserved the promotion.

But first things first. She and Aiden were both being considered individually to lead a huge upcoming campaign for the St. Raphael Resort, an exclusive matchmaking retreat that catered to singles looking to find love—a multi-million dollar campaign that came with a generous, five-figure bonus and would elevate their standing within the firm, as well as in the advertising industry. If Chloe nailed today's presentation for Organic Kitty, she was fairly optimistic that she'd be assigned the St. Raphael Resort account. From there, it was a logical leap to the senior executive position.

She smiled to herself as they waited for the next available elevator, enjoying those visions of grandeur dancing in her head. As much as she liked Aiden, as a person and a coworker, her own competitive streak drove her to succeed—on her own, and without relying on anyone else to get her there.

With the morning crowd finally thinned out, the next elevator enabled them to step on board without feeling crushed. She and Aiden ended up in the back. Standing so close to him, she could feel the heat of his body. And God, he always smelled so damned delicious, like sandalwood and fresh, clean citrus. Whatever his cologne, it was like breathing in a tempting aphrodisiac that never failed to arouse her womanly senses.

After stopping on various floors to let other people out, they finally arrived at the thirty-second floor, which opened directly into the reception area of Perry & Associates.

"Break a leg today, Chloe," Aiden said, winking at her.

She laughed at his choice of words. "Don't you wish."

They parted ways, and as soon as Aiden was out of

sight, her thoughts returned to the Organic Kitty presentation and how she intended to win over the client.

AIDEN SAT AT the back of the conference room, along with a few other colleagues, silently watching as Chloe worked her magic in wooing the higher-ups at Organic Kitty with her stellar campaign. She'd focused on giving the company a much needed boost to their consumer visibility through new branding and a catchy slogan. Her voice was strong and engaging as she spoke, and her PowerPoint slides showcased a multitude of innovative advertising ideas, clever marketing and social media strategies focused toward elevating the Kitty brand, as well as attracting new buyers.

The clients were riveted by her persuasive and appealing presentation. Aiden was riveted by the woman herself. As always, she was confident, commanding and in control, traits he found sexy as hell. Today she was wearing a conservative, but feminine skirted suit in navy blue, a professional choice for her meeting with clients. The cream silk blouse layered beneath the tailored jacket hinted at a softer, more sensual side, as did the peek of lace from the camisole she wore.

His gaze traveled down the length of her body, to the fitted skirt that hugged the curve of her hips and rounded bottom and ended just below the knee. From there, she had a fantastic pair of long, slender legs that most of the men in the firm took the time to notice as she walked by, probably because of the four inch heels she always opted to wear—the kind that made guys think of sex and sin, and doing both with her while she kept them on.

Yeah, he was definitely guilty of utilizing that fantasy a time or two, and now was *not* the time or place to let his thoughts wander in that direction. Shifting subtly in his seat, he glanced back up at her pretty face. Her rich, dark brown hair was pulled back into a sleek, sophisticated ponytail, and her bright hazel eyes were more green than brown at the moment. Her enthusiastic expression matched the same infectious energy infusing her voice and body language, adding a nice little punch to her very compelling sales pitch. It was clear to anyone who watched Chloe that she was incredibly passionate about her work, as well as the advertising campaign she'd created for Organic Kitty.

While Aiden was highly attracted to Chloe on several different levels, her utter focus, control and drive when it came to advancing in the corporate world reminded him of his ex-wife and how her ambition had eventually destroyed their marriage, and his trust. Paige had refused to allow anything to get in the way of her success as a defense attorney, not even an unplanned pregnancy that she'd made clear she never wanted. A pregnancy she'd terminated without any discussion or input from him.

The end result of what she'd done in order to pursue her professional goals still cut Aiden deeper than a knife and had shattered his illusions of love and commitment, and the sanctuary of marriage. After their bitter divorce three years ago, he'd vowed that he'd never get seriously involved with another career-minded woman again. No, the next time he put a ring on someone's finger, he'd be damned sure she was on the same page as him when it came to the importance of family.

Career-wise, Aiden recognized that Chloe and Paige had a lot in common. But while his wife had been cold and calculating, Chloe was the complete opposite. Chloe was undoubtedly driven to succeed, but having worked with her for the past two years, he also knew she was warm, genuine and friendly. Most important, she respected her colleagues and had a great reputation in the industry—two exceptional qualities that were hard to find in such a cut-throat business.

But damned if he wasn't overwhelmingly attracted to her, despite the many reasons why he shouldn't want her. He'd be a liar if he said all that confidence and sass of hers didn't do it for him in a major way. Sexually, he liked a woman a little on the aggressive side, a woman who knew what she liked and wasn't afraid to challenge him in the bedroom. Judging by their seductive flirtations and Chloe's determined attitude when it came to getting what she wanted, Aiden highly suspected she was *exactly* that kind of woman.

Not that he'd ever have the pleasure of discovering for himself what kind of lover she was. Resisting Chloe and the tempting awareness between them was paramount, not only because of the no dating policy the company enforced, but because Aiden was fairly certain she was seeing someone—some guy he'd seen her with a few times down at the Executive Bar after work. Besides, even if she wasn't dating someone else, Aiden wasn't about to risk a career opportunity that was so close to being within his grasp by having an office affair that ended up damaging his future plans to start up his own ad agency.

Right now, his sole focus was on acquiring the multi-million dollar St. Raphael Resort account, because the substantial bonus that was being dangled as an incentive was exactly what he needed to fund his new venture. It was between himself and Chloe as to who would be assigned to St. Raphael, and considering the exceptional job she was doing on the Organic Kitty campaign today, there was no doubt in Aiden's mind that the competition for the resort account was going to be fierce. Making the choice between him and his office rival for the job was going to be very difficult indeed.

Chloe wrapped up her PowerPoint spiel, and it was evident that the client loved her ideas and was eager to implement them. Perry, the owner and CEO of the firm, had been present during the sales pitch, and he appeared equally pleased with her campaign. Right on the spot, Organic Kitty agreed to sign on with Perry & Associates, and Chloe's surprise and delight made Aiden smile. He knew how amazing it felt to close a deal. The adrenaline rush of victory and the high of success was *almost* as good as sex.

With the presentation over, he stood up to leave the conference room, and on his way out he gently grabbed Chloe's arm to get her attention for a moment. She glanced up at him, her hazel eyes bright with exhilaration, and her face flushed with the sheer joy of success. Her pink, glossy lips were curved into a delightful smile, and damn if he didn't want to kiss that luscious mouth and discover if she tasted as good as he imagined she would.

He cleared his throat and released his hold on her arm. "Nice job, Reiss," he told her, meaning it. "I don't even like cats and you made me want to buy their product."

She laughed at his attempt at humor. "Then I've done my job."

"Very well, it seems." He briefly looked over at the happy client who was busy shaking Perry's hand while gushing about the campaign, then back at Chloe. "Congratulations on the new account."

Her gaze warmed with appreciation. "Thanks, Aiden."

That was another thing he liked about Chloe. Despite her creative talent and advertising savvy, she displayed absolutely no conceit or arrogance over her newest triumph, as many of their coworkers did. She didn't feel the need to flaunt or brag about her acquisitions, and to Aiden, that spoke to her confidence and determination when it came to pleasing her client.

Her success today was a nice feather in her cap and put her another notch closer to a promotion and taking on bigger accounts, but Aiden wasn't too worried. There was no denying that Chloe was good at her job, but he'd like to think that he was better. The proof would come as soon as he was awarded the St. Rafael account.

"How about I buy you a drink later, after work, to celebrate?" he offered.

She nodded, and smiled. "Yeah, I'd like that."

Knowing she and Perry had contract details to go over with the client, Aiden left the conference room and went to his office to return some phone calls and to work on a few accounts that needed his attention. He skipped going out for lunch, and instead bought a roast beef sandwich from the lunch cart to eat while he answered emails and edited copy for a client's upcoming media blitz.

At three-fifteen in the afternoon, the phone on his desk buzzed and Perry's personal secretary, Lena, spoke through the intercom. "Aiden, Mr. Perry would like to see you in his office regarding the St. Raphael account, please."

A jolt of excitement surged through Aiden. *This was it,* he thought, tamping down the crazy urge to execute an elated fist pump in the air. Despite Chloe's fantastic campaign today, Perry was going to entrust *him* with one of the firm's biggest clients—and as soon as he blew away St. Raphael with a kick-ass campaign, that five-figure bonus would be all his. *Yes!*

"I'll be right there, Lena," he said, his voice much calmer than he felt inside.

After disconnecting the call, he stood and put his suit jacket back on to look as professional as possible, straightened his tie and started toward Perry's suite of executive offices. On the way, he caught sight of Chloe across the way, heading in the same direction. Her smile faded, as did his, as they both came to a stop at the double glass doors that led to Perry's domain.

"Wait a second," he said, unable to stop the unease settling in his stomach like lead. "Where are *you* going?"

"To see Perry." She looked equally wary, as if seeing him there had taken her by surprise, as well. "And you?"

"The same." *Shit.* This situation didn't bode well. Not at all. "Did he want to talk to you about the St. Raphael account, too?"

A slight frown creased her brow. "Yes."

Aiden had no idea what was up, because they were each qualified and experienced enough to handle the account on their own. Chloe was coming off the high of her Organic Kitty presentation earlier today, which was no doubt fresh in Perry's mind and could possibly give her an added edge. But honestly, there was no telling what the CEO had planned, or why he'd summoned them both. Unless he intended to give one of them the account, and let the other one down easy, all in one fell swoop.

It wouldn't be the first time something like that had happened in his career—and he hated that he was in that position now.

He exhaled a deep breath, refusing to let Chloe see him sweat because he hadn't lost the account yet—and wouldn't let it slip through his fingers if he had his way. Pushing open the glass door, he gave her an easygoing smile and waved a hand inside the executive offices. "After you."

2

CHLOE SAT DOWN in one of the plush seats in front of Richard Perry's large glass-topped desk, and Aiden settled into the chair next to hers, while their boss regarded them both with an unreadable expression.

A nearly tangible tension vibrated in the air between her and Aiden. There was so much at stake, for the both of them, and she reminded herself that confidence, sprinkled with a large dose of fortitude, was the key to getting what she wanted. That way of thinking had served her well for most of her adult life, and certainly during her career as an advertising executive.

If she didn't count her horrible lapse in judgment with her ex-fiancé, Neil, four years ago that had nearly cost her everything, personally and professionally, and made her realize that she wasn't so different from her mother after all. That despite the goals she'd set for herself and her vow to never let a man control her life and decisions, she'd failed miserably. Her screwed-up relationship with Neil made it abundantly clear that her judgment when it came to men sucked.

But *unlike* her mother, she refused to make the same mistake twice. Dropping her guard and allowing herself to get involved with a man on an emotional level was no longer an option for her. Now she put all her time and energy into her career, which fulfilled her in all the ways that mattered—except one. But for those times when she had a sexual itch to scratch, well, that's where friends with benefits came in handy. It was an arrangement that worked well for all involved, but mostly, for her. No mess, no fuss, and nothing to interfere with her main pursuit of climbing the corporate ladder straight to the top.

And right now, there was only one thing standing in the way of her stepping up another rung and getting the St. Raphael account—Aiden Landry, the man who'd also been called to Perry's office. But she'd just proven her worth to Perry that morning, and hopefully her ability to completely overhaul a company's advertising and marketing plan was still fresh in his mind and would provide her an advantage over Aiden.

That was her hope, anyways, but she had to admit it was a bit unsettling to be sitting right next to her biggest competition in the firm, a guy who wanted this account just as badly as she did. Only one of them would get the job, and a quick glance at Aiden told her that he had that confident look about him, too—backed by an impressive amount of determination.

Refusing to be the least bit intimidated, she gathered her composure, crossed her legs, clasped her hands in her lap and waited for their boss, a distinguished-looking man in his early sixties, to address them.

"I'm sure you're wondering why you're both here," Richard Perry said a moment later as he glanced from Aiden, to her, direct and businesslike. "And I'm not going to drag this out any longer than necessary. Bottom line, the partners and I couldn't decide which one of you deserved the St. Raphael account more. You're both incredibly innovative and have outstanding success rates with your current accounts. Since there is so much riding on this campaign, in this instance we've decided that two creative minds will give the firm a better advantage, than one."

Chloe was so taken aback by Richard's announcement that she didn't know what to say. All the hopes she'd harbored in regards to her career and a big promotion dwindled in that moment.

Aiden didn't seem thrilled about the new arrangement, either, not when they'd been expecting a solo mission. "So, we'll be working *together* on the St. Raphael account?" he asked, a cautious note to his voice.

"No, you'll be working separately, in *lead* positions," Richard clarified as he reclined in his leather chair, looking completely at ease even though he'd just delivered a one-two punch to her and Aiden. "You'll each be assigned your own marketing team to help you with your campaign, and you'll each give the client a full presentation, along with a complete advertising and promotional package geared toward developing the resort's matchmaking brand. They're open to restructuring their activities at the resort to make the social interaction between couples more appealing, and they'd like to see ways to increase their profit margin, while still giving their targeted consumer a great overall experience."

Oh, wow. The project was huge and complex, and clearly Perry wanted to see which one of them could better deal with the stress and mental challenge of such an enormous task—the same kind of pressures that would face a senior executive. Chloe was more than capable of handling the assignment, and although the man sitting next to her was equally qualified, she wasn't going to let that fact mess with her head.

Richard steepled his fingers in front of him, and continued, "I think it will be interesting to have two separate campaigns for this particular client, one from a female perspective, and one from a male perspective. But you both also need to be aware that there is another ad agency that will be vying for the resort's account, which makes it all the more important that the two of you come up with some kind of unique marketing twist to your presentations to edge out the rival company. Two separate campaigns from each of you gives our firm twice the advantage, however, only one of you will be awarded the account, based on which, if any, campaign the client chooses."

So, in essence, she and Aiden were being dealt a double whammy. Not only were they in competition with each other, they also had the added competition of another agency soliciting the account, as well.

Curious to know what Aiden thought of this new twist, Chloe cast him a quick, sidelong glance. The man was good at hiding his emotions. His poker face gave her no indication of how he was feeling about the two of them being directly pitted against one another, and she supposed he was smart not to give her any kind of advantage, just as she had no intention of letting her own frustration show.

"In order to create the best presentation and campaign possible, you've both been invited to St. Raphael to experience the resort's amenities and atmosphere for yourselves," Richard said as he reached for a butterscotch drop in the crystal bowl on his desk—his favorite type of hard candy he usually grazed on in the afternoon as a sweet treat. He unwrapped the confection and slipped it into his mouth, sucking on the candy for a few seconds before speaking again.

"Fully immersing yourself in the experience will give you a better idea of what works, what doesn't and what the resort needs to change or elevate in terms of quality, service and overall customer satisfaction."

Aiden rubbed a hand along his tense jaw. "So, you want us to go through the matchmaking process along with everyone else registered at the resort?" he asked their boss.

"Just go through the motions, Landry," Perry said with a casual wave of his hand. "You're not there to find the love of your life, but you can't create an effective campaign without knowing what you're up against. In this case, there are millions of dollars on the line. The other firm's executives will be there, as well, so I trust that you both can handle the situation and what you're required to do?"

Perry's request was more of a subtle challenge than a question, and Chloe wasn't about to voice her own aversion to mingling with other desperate singles and risk being replaced by another hungry ad executive who'd kill to have the opportunity she was being given. This wouldn't be the first time she'd stepped into the dirty trenches to get the job done, and if she had to endure organized activities, fend off unwanted advances and make small talk with men who'd been deemed compatible for her, well, then, she was willing to suffer for her career.

"Absolutely, Mr. Perry," she said in a tone as unwavering as her commitment to the firm, and the campaign.

Aiden's reply was just as resolute. "Yes, sir."

"Good." Richard gave a curt nod, pleased to have them both on board. "You'll be leaving a week from Monday, so make sure you have all your other accounts covered before you go. Good luck to both of you."

With that, Perry let them go, and she and Aiden walked in silence back toward the outer offices. As soon as they stepped through the double glass doors, Chloe came to a stop and so did Aiden, both of them still processing everything that had just happened back in Richard's office.

Aiden gave his head a hard shake. "I didn't see *that* coming," he muttered.

"Me, either," she agreed. She'd anticipated that one of them would have been celebrating right now, preferably her. Instead, there was another firm involved and she and Aiden were now adversaries of sorts, each one of them motivated to do whatever might be necessary to create the winning campaign and outshine the other, while spending a week together at a matchmaking resort.

While they'd always had a great working relationship, they'd never been set against one another, and she hated to think that their drive and ambition to secure this client, and the generous bonus, might ruin their friendly rapport.

She glanced up at Aiden, meeting his vivid gaze, momentarily struck by how mesmerizing those blue orbs could be. "Promise me something?" she blurted out, before she could think better of what she was about to ask. Or why it was so important to her. It just *was.*

"Sure," he said, taking her request very seriously.

Exhaling a deep breath, she put her concerns out in the open before she changed her mind. "Promise me when everything is said and done, if one of us ultimately gets the St. Raphael account, it won't change our working relationship. Or our friendship," she added, because she definitely considered him that, too.

He tipped his head, a reassuring smile on his lips. "You should know by now that I don't operate that way, or hold professional grudges."

She knew that to be true, but his words relieved her, anyway. "I don't, either," she said, and allowed a sassy grin to surface, as well as her competitive nature. "But I hate to see a grown man cry, and I'm sure you'll be reduced to tears when I'm awarded the campaign."

Aiden chuckled, clearly amused with her prediction. "Chloe, Chloe, Chloe," he chided in a deep voice as smooth as aged whiskey, and just as intoxicating. "Just for the record, I have absolutely *no* intention of losing, to the other firm, or to you."

Now this, a direct challenge, she could handle. "We could spend the rest of the night arguing over that, but let's make this short and simple. May the best woman win." She extended her hand toward him.

His much larger hand engulfed hers in a sensual warmth that traveled all the way up her arm, and he leaned in close, his eyes dancing with his own brand of wit and daring. "With the emphasis on *man,* though I'm sure it'll be a fight to the finish."

She withdrew her hand from his, doing her best to ignore the heat and awareness his touch had so effortlessly aroused in her. "Oh, yeah, you can count on that."

Game on.

"SO, WHAT BRINGS YOU to my neck of the woods?" Sam Landry, Aiden's younger brother by two years, eyed him curiously across the scarred wooden table where they were seated at McGann's Pub in downtown Boston. "Don't you usually spend your Friday evenings at that fancy Executive Bar where you work, schmoozing with colleagues?"

Aiden grinned at Sam's exaggerated description as he lifted his cold bottle of Guinness to his lips for a drink, enjoying the taste of the dark, rich stout. His brother, a P.I., never missed an opportunity to rib Aiden about his white-collar profession, especially since it was such a departure from the proud family tradition.

Their grandfather had been a decorated cop for the Boston Police Department, then their father, Jack, followed by Sam—until his brother had been shot on the job and the injury had forced him to reevaluate his career and future. Even though Sam no longer worked for BPD, he was still entrenched in the business as a private investigator who often used his past connections with the force to help him in the current cases he worked on.

Everyone had assumed that Aiden would carry the same torch for justice and head off to the police academy once he graduated college. Instead, he'd shocked everyone when he made the decision to major in advertising and marketing over criminal justice his junior year. The big difference between him and Sam was that Aiden loved the creative aspect of his career, while his brother preferred the constant movement of chasing bad guys and the unexpected twists that came with detective work.

While Aiden's parents had always been supportive about his choice of job and his accomplishments, he knew he'd initially disappointed his father by venturing outside the realm of law enforcement. And being the so-called black sheep who'd strayed from family expectations, it made him an easy target for his brother's good-natured needling, which he'd grown used to.

Aiden set his bottle of beer back on the table and shot Sam a halfhearted look of irritation. "Do you always have to give me shit because I sometimes prefer a good beer over aged Scotch and want to visit with you?"

"Yeah, I do, because it doesn't happen often," his brother answered, his gaze flickering with amusement. "I gotta get my licks in where I can."

Aiden just shook his head, because despite their differences in personality and profession, and his brother's penchant for busting his chops, he and Sam had always been close. Aiden, being the firstborn, was far more serious than his carefree, easygoing sibling, but there was no denying that beyond the bond of being brothers, they were also best friends. And now, with their parents retired and living in Florida, he appreciated his relationship with Sam even more.

The truth was, after today's shake-up at the office, Aiden just wanted to relax and unwind, without the added pressure of smiling and laughing with colleagues when he wasn't in the mood. He'd even promised Chloe a drink to celebrate her new account with Organic Kitty, but he'd have to make it up to her another time. She was another distraction he didn't want to deal with tonight, not when he was still trying to process the fact that they'd gone from being coworkers to rivals vying for the same account.

"Whatever is bugging you, get it off your chest already," Sam said, pulling him out of his thoughts. "That brooding look is going to scare off the women. Oh, wait, your uptight business suit already did that." He smirked.

Aiden laughed, giving his brother the reaction he'd been angling for. True, he stood out in a place where the dress code was jeans and T-shirt casual, which was all Sam ever wore. "Then it's a good thing I'm not here to pick up women."

"Yeah, well, you're cramping my style," Sam grumbled, and gazed longingly at two pretty females sitting a few tables away who were giving Sam an equally interested look. Leaning forward in his seat, Aiden braced his arms on the table, figuring it might help to talk to Sam about what had happened today at the office, as he'd suggested. "Actually, I have some news I need to get off my chest. Do you remember me telling you about the big account I was hoping to get?"

Sam thought for a moment, then asked, "The one for that singles, matchmaking resort?"

Aiden nodded. "Yeah, that's the one."

"Are we here to celebrate?" Sam asked hopefully, already tipping his beer for a premature toast.

"No, not yet." Aiden released a heavy sigh. "I found out today that not only is another ad firm vying for the job, but Perry decided to assign Chloe and I to the account. Not to work together, but to come up with separate campaigns for the resort. He wants a male and female perspective. Whoever's campaign the client chooses will be awarded the account."

Sam's eyes widened in surprise. "So you have to compete directly *against* Chloe for the account?"

"Yep." His troubled tone echoed the way he felt about the entire situation.

Over the past two years of working at Perry & Associates, Aiden had spoken about Chloe numerous times to Sam, saying how much he respected her as a colleague. His brother had also met and talked to—or rather *flirted* with—Chloe the one and only time Sam had stopped by the Executive Bar to have a drink with Aiden, so Sam was familiar enough with their working relationship to know just how bothered Aiden was that the two of them were now adversaries. However, Aiden had promised Chloe that he wouldn't let this campaign ruin their friendship, and he was determined to make sure he held true to their pact.

"I'm sorry, bro." Sam gave a sympathetic shake of his head. "That plain sucks."

"Tell me about it." Aiden finished off his beer, and if he didn't have to get in a car and drive, he would have ordered a double scotch. He certainly needed one.

They sat in silence for a few minutes, the Friday night crowd in McGann's growing louder as the bar filled up with patrons. Women walked by in skimpy outfits, giving both him and his brother a lingering glance that made it clear they were more than interested in a good time, but Aiden wasn't. When he glanced across the table at Sam, there was no mistaking the sly grin on his lips and the mischievous look in his eyes.

Aiden narrowed his gaze, wondering what his brother found so amusing. "What?"

"You're not going to let a *girl* win, are you?" Sam asked, an all too familiar taunting note to his voice. It was the same one he'd used to goad Aiden into doing things he shouldn't, all throughout their childhood.

"Hell, no." Aiden considered himself a gentleman, but this was a competition between two coworkers, and all bets were off. Girl or no, his kick-ass campaign was going to earn him the St. Raphael account.

"Good." Despite Sam's succinct tone, his lips were still twitching with mirth. "I don't want you to go all soft because your competition is smoking hot and lust is clouding your feeble brain."

Aiden blinked in shock at his brother. "Excuse me?" What the hell did Sam know about his attraction to Chloe?

"Oh, come on, Aiden," Sam said with a laugh as he tipped his chair back on its hind legs. "I'm not deaf, dumb or blind. I only saw the two of you together once, at that highbrow bar of yours, and the chemistry between the two of you was pretty damn obvious."

Aiden shrugged off his brother's claim. "It's just a friendly flirtation."

Sam lifted a dubious brow. "Except for the way you stared at her ass when she walked away from our table. I can guarantee that the thoughts in your head involving that sweet backside of hers were indecent and downright kinky."

He shrugged and didn't even try to deny the truth. "She's got a great ass. So sue me for appreciating all its finer qualities."

A wide grin curved Sam's mouth. "Good to know your libido isn't dead. I was starting to worry."

"My sex drive is fine, thank you very much." But Aiden had to admit he hadn't seen much action lately, by his own choice. His main focus was his job, and ultimately grabbing the brass ring of opening his own ad agency in the near future. And in order to achieve that goal, he had to win the account.

"So how long are you going to resist the attraction between you and Chloe?" Sam asked, as persistent and pushy as ever. "I got the impression if you made a move, she could be easily persuaded."

For Sam, being with a woman was that simple. Not so much for Aiden. "We're both professionals, working for the same ad agency, and we're not going to risk our careers for sex."

Sam rolled his eyes dramatically. "Jesus, Aiden, who says you have to risk anything? It's just feel-good *sex,* not a lifetime commitment. Besides, the risk of getting caught could give the affair an added element of excitement."

That's exactly how *Sam* operated…getting laid was all about having a good time without any strings attached. It hadn't always been that way, and while Aiden understood his brother's perspective on sex and women and keeping his emotions out of the equation, Aiden's views were much different, despite his ex-wife's betrayal. He'd never been the love 'em and leave 'em type, and that hadn't changed after his divorce. If anything, he'd become more discriminating when it came to women and relationships. And yeah, sex, too.

"Don't you ever want something more than just a string of one-night stands?" Aiden asked his brother.

Sam gaped at him, as if he'd spoken blasphemy.

"You're kidding me, right? We both thought we had something *more,* and look how well that turned out for us."

Not well at all. "Okay, point taken," Aiden said. Being burned by a woman had left Sam jaded and uneasy about trusting again. But even though Aiden's marriage had been less than ideal, he liked to believe that there was a woman out there for him. But he knew that Chloe wasn't that woman. She was too career-oriented to be anything more than a passing affair. And even *that* wasn't an option for him.

"Hey, Sam," a soft feminine voice called out, pulling Aiden out of his thoughts.

One of the women that had been sitting a few tables away now stood in front of them, gazing down at Sam with a sultry smile on her lips while her fingers lightly touched his shoulder. She was young and pretty, and wore a tight-fitting dress that accentuated all her best assets. She had Sam's full attention.

"Denise and I were wondering if you and your friend wanted to join us?" She bit her lip seductively as she glanced briefly at Aiden, then back at Sam again. "We can pull up an extra chair or two, if you'd like."

"I'd love to, Carol," Sam looked at Aiden, his raised brow silently asking if he was going to accompany them.

This was Sam's scene, not Aiden's. He shook his head and tried to appear regretful. "Thanks for the invite, but I need to get going."

"Okay," Carol said, not at all disappointed, since clearly it was Sam she wanted. "We'll save a seat for you, Sam." She sashayed back to her table, a deliberate sway to her hips—all for Sam's benefit, which he openly enjoyed.

Aiden chuckled and stood up, along with his brother. "Looks like someone's getting lucky tonight."

"Jealous?" Sam grinned.

Pulling out his wallet, Aiden tossed enough cash on the table to cover their drinks and leave a decent tip. "Not at all," he said, meaning it. "By the way, just so you know, I'll be leaving next Monday for the Bahamas, where the St. Raphael resort is located."

"Is Chloe going, too?"

"Yes, we're both going." He tucked his wallet back into his pocket, and knowing exactly what his brother was thinking, Aiden attempted to cut him off at the pass. "It's a *business* trip, Sam."

"Which also presents the perfect opportunity for the two of you to take advantage of your attraction, in a place where no one would ever be the wiser." Sam waggled his brows suggestively.

"Not gonna happen."

Sam released an exasperated sigh. "You know what your problem is? You're way too uptight. And you've been that way since your divorce."

"I'm not uptight. I'm careful and discreet."

"Like I said. You're *uptight*." Sam slapped him on the back in brotherly camaraderie. "Loosen up and live a little, bro. You might be surprised how much fun you can have when you're not being so damned serious."

With that bit of advice, his brother walked away, leaving Aiden to ponder the wisdom of Sam's comments. Or the lack thereof.

3

THE FOLLOWING MONDAY at seven in the morning, Chloe was seated next to Aiden on a plane heading to Nassau in the Bahamas. From there, they'd take a small puddle jumper to the island of St. Raphael where the private, secluded resort was located. They were scheduled to arrive at the hotel by early afternoon. Once the jet leveled out, the pilot announced that it was now okay to move about the cabin and turn on approved electronic devices, and promised that the refreshment cart would be making its way down the aisle shortly.

Chloe frequently took business trips for work and was used to sitting by the window in the cramped quarters of coach, usually next to a stranger who kept to themselves for the duration of the flight. But the moment Aiden plopped his big body into the chair beside hers and their knees and elbows bumped as they buckled their lap belts, she knew their intimate seating arrangements would wreak havoc with every one of her five senses for the next few hours.

So far, her prediction proved to be true. Sitting next to the window, her body was hyper aware of his broad shoulder brushing against her arm and the way his leg occasionally grazed her thigh when he shifted in his seat to find a comfortable position that would accommodate his long legs. At least he'd settled down for takeoff, and as she cast a sidelong glance at him, she found herself envious of his ability to completely relax when the surface of her skin buzzed with sensual awareness.

His head was resting against the back of his seat, and though his eyes were closed, she wasn't sure if he was sleeping or not. But even like this, he was hotter than any man had a right to be with his early morning tousled hair, the sweep of his ridiculously long, dark lashes against his cheeks, and those full lips that were made to give a woman all kinds of forbidden pleasures. Even his casual attire made him look sexy and confidently male.

She'd never seen him in anything but a business suit, and she had to admit that he looked damn fine in a dark blue short-sleeved knit shirt that complimented his toned physique, and a pair of well-worn jeans that lovingly clung to his muscular thighs and other interesting body parts that piqued her interest. And why did he always have to smell so damned good? His expensive cologne was subtle, but the warm, sandalwood scent, mixed with his own male pheromones, never failed to tap into her desires and make her ache deep inside.

At the office, she was constantly near Aiden, but with work as her top priority she was able to keep her attraction to him in check. Or walk away when that heady pull between them became too overwhelming. But right here, right now, there was no putting distance between herself and Aiden, so she was just going to have to suck it up and deal.

Lord, it was going to be a long flight.

Desperately needing some kind of distraction, she reached down and pulled a folder from the computer bag she'd stowed beneath the chair in front of her. Releasing the fold-down tray, she set the file on top and immersed herself in work. Specifically, the research she'd already compiled on the St. Raphael resort and its current branding, mission statement and operating procedures.

Unlike a singles resort, where the main draw was drinking and partying in a girls/guys gone wild style, and hooking up with the opposite sex was a free-for-all, St. Raphael offered a unique and modern-day spin to matching compatible couples while offering fun, interactive activities in a romantic atmosphere. While the concept didn't interest Chloe on a personal level, from an advertising angle it was an executive's dream. There were so many interesting aspects to build a campaign on, like developing a catchy slogan to pull in consumers, beautiful pictures to capture their imagination, and the lure of finding love and a happily ever after.

She and Aiden had already filled out the required questionnaire that the resort used to match up couples, and the two of them were scheduled to attend events and various activities to mix and mingle and "make a connection." It was the only way for them to evaluate the process in order to present the client with a cohesive advertising campaign for the resort. Perry had even hired a local professional photographer to be on hand to capture any shots she or Aiden needed to elevate their presentation.

There was no way Chloe could forget that this was a business trip with a huge incentive on the line. But she also knew in order to really absorb everything the resort had to offer, she had to open herself up to the fun, seductive aspect of the island retreat so she could better translate the experience into her campaign.

And that included relaxing around Aiden, too. They weren't at the office, and there was absolutely no harm in a little flirtation between them, which they already indulged in, anyway. And if her seductive teasing threw him off his game a bit, well, it would be his own fault for letting their attraction get the best of him.

"We're not even at the resort yet, and you're already working?"

The low, chiding voice came from Aiden, who was no longer dozing. She glanced at him, meeting his dark, velvet blue gaze, still heavy-lidded from his brief nap. "I started a portfolio for notes and ideas for my campaign as soon as Perry announced we'd each be doing a presentation. Do you know what the name St. Raphael stands for?" she asked, testing his knowledge of the resort.

A slow, lazy smile curved those sinful lips of his. "St. Raphael is the patron saint of love and lovers, which is very appropriate for a matchmaking resort."

The husky way he said the word *lovers* sent a warm shiver through her. Yeah, flirting with him was very natural and easy and always reciprocated with genuine interest. "I'm impressed. You've obviously done your homework, too." She would have been more shocked if he hadn't.

"I always do," he murmured. "Speaking of homework, how crazy was that matchmaking questionnaire we had to fill out?" he asked with an incredulous shake of his head.

The required survey had been a long, tedious process that had covered every end of the spectrum of a person's life, from personality, career aspirations, religion, finances, pet peeves, family values and even sexual compatibility. That last part had been her favorite section of the test. As she'd answered each question, her mind had strayed to Aiden, wondering if his responses had matched hers. Was he more gentle and romantic in the bedroom, or did he prefer the aggression of unleashed passion? Was he open to role-playing and fulfilling fantasies if his partner was willing? And how important was foreplay to him?

Oh, yeah, she'd definitely had fun with those questions. The other more personal ones, not so much, but she'd been honest with her replies in order to see how the whole matchmaking process worked.

"The quiz was pretty intensive," she agreed, and since he was in a chatty mood she slipped her work folder back into her computer case. "I felt like I was back in college taking a final exam. Except the subject was my life. I know the questionnaire is necessary, but it all seems so...desperate and forced."

He absently rubbed his palms along his jean-clad thighs, considering her reply for a moment. "How so?"

Since he looked genuinely curious to hear her opinion, she gave it to him. "I'm not a big fan of professional matchmaking," she said honestly. "I'd rather let nature take it's course instead of my interest in someone being dictated by the answers on a quiz." After how badly her last relationship ended, for her, basic chemistry was the way to go, without any messy emotions to lead her astray. And it gave *her* more control over how long an affair lasted.

"Which also has its pros and cons," he refuted smoothly, not the least bit bothered by the rattle of the plane as it hit an air pocket. "The problem with letting the relationship develop naturally and being lured in by the initial physical attraction is that you only see what's on the surface and you don't really know the person beyond the basic likes and dislikes."

She tipped her head to the side, always enjoying a good debate with Aiden, knowing that the deeper they got into this conversation, the more her point would be revealed. When he believed strongly in something, his fierce passion, drive and intelligence was always a delightful sight to behold. "And you think a matchmaking quiz would change that?"

"I think the test might reveal some potential problems between couples that might not be there in the beginning, but could cause issues and conflict once the initial glow wears off. Or even after marriage."

Something in his gaze hardened with that last sentence. Aiden was always so charming and easy-going, that the darker emotion she saw flicker in his eyes startled her.

"I think it's important to know if you have a similar outlook on politics as someone you're seriously dating," Aiden went on, as if choosing his words carefully. "Or if your views on finances are the same. Or what kind of priority having kids and a family is in comparison to career aspirations."

"I see your point, but I also think the results could be skewed, depending on the answers the other person provides," she disputed lightly. She knew Aiden was divorced, and wondered if his argument was based on his own personal experience. "I highly doubt that someone is going to openly state on the application that they're a controlling jerk, or that they have severe OCD tendencies or if they have an internet porn addiction."

He grinned at that, his demeanor relaxing once again. "Okay, I'm not saying it's a perfect system, but statistics do show that taking a compatibility test does work and can identify issues between couples *before* things get serious. And that's not a bad thing."

Chloe doubted that a quiz would have alerted her to Neil's dominating behavior and his explosive temper when things didn't go his way. No, it wasn't until he'd put an engagement ring on her finger that she'd started to see the true personality he'd kept under wraps while they'd been dating. "Well, it's a good thing that I'm not looking for anything serious, anytime soon," she said, pulling herself back from those dark thoughts.

A slight frown marred his brows. "What about the guy you've been seeing?"

She hadn't been seriously involved with anyone in years, and had no idea what had given him the impression she was seeing anyone, let alone seriously. "What are you talking about?"

"That guy I've seen you with at the Executive Bar," he explained, and then she understood. "I just assumed the two of you were dating."

"Ummm, no." An occasional hookup didn't equate to dating. Steve, the guy Aiden was referring to, had been nothing more than a friend with benefits. Neither of them had been interested in a complicated relationship, until Steve had met Jenna and he'd fallen hard for the other woman. That had put an end to their booty calls, and Chloe hadn't been with anyone since.

"I'm not seeing anyone," she said, deciding to keep her reply simple and straightforward. And now that the question was out there in the open, she was curious to know if he was dating anyone. "How about you?"

"Nope." He shook his head. "I've been so focused on work that I haven't had time for a relationship."

A relationship, no. But what about sex, she wondered, just as the refreshment cart came to a stop by their seats. She couldn't imagine a sexy, virile man like Aiden abstaining for long stretches of time. But as she hadn't volunteered that information, she couldn't ask him, either.

The pretty female flight attendant turned their way. "Would either of you like something to drink?" she asked, her gaze lingering appreciatively on Aiden.

Aiden didn't seem to notice the attention as he glanced at Chloe with an impish smile. "I believe I still owe you a drink to celebrate the Organic Kitty contract," he said, sounding truly apologetic for not showing up at the Executive Bar like he'd promised. "Can I make it up to you now?"

"It's kinda early for alcohol," she said, her tone wry.

"Coffee then?"

She nodded. "Sure." She could use a shot of caffeine since she'd been out of the house early to catch their flight.

Aiden asked for two coffees, hers with cream and sugar, and just sugar for his. The attendant filled the order, placed the paper cups on their trays along with a warm cinnamon roll for a morning snack, then moved on to the next row.

"I think you're getting off way too easy for standing me up," she said, motioning to the *free* coffee she was sipping. "I waited for two hours that evening and you never showed. The least you could have done was text me to let me know you weren't coming."

His grimace reflected a genuine amount of contrition. "I really am sorry about that. I was just so thrown by Perry's decision to pit us against each other, I needed time to process it all."

"I get it," she said as she pulled off a piece of her cinnamon roll and popped it into her mouth. "Honestly, I felt the same way."

"But I'm fine now," he reassured her with a grin while biting into his own breakfast pastry. "In fact, I'm looking forward to the challenge."

"That's good, because you're going *down,* Landry," she said with a playful, flirtatious growl that sounded very suggestive, even to her own ears. Her innocent comment had twisted into a sexual innuendo that hung in the air between them like a challenge of its own.

"Mmm, we'll see about that," he murmured.

His eyes had turned dark and hot, and something

deep inside Chloe quivered with awareness. After what seemed like an endless amount of time, he finally glanced away, took a drink of his coffee and devoured the rest of his cinnamon roll before she'd even finished half of hers.

Not quite ready to let the slow burn between them fade away, she decided to embrace her new go-with-it attitude and have a little fun with Aiden. "So, back to that questionnaire we filled out. How important is sexual compatibility to you in a relationship?"

Aiden's bemused expression told her that he had no qualms discussing the intimate details of his sexual preferences with her, and it was that playful, comfortable attitude she enjoyed so much about him. They could pretty much talk about anything and it never felt awkward.

"On a scale of one to ten, I'd rate it a nine. I have a healthy sexual appetite and I'd like my partner to match that. You?"

She'd always pegged him for a man who went the distance, in *everything* he did. Including sex, it seemed, and that enticing thought had her nipples tightening against the confines of her lace bra. "Oh, definitely a nine for me, too," she murmured, even knowing they were playing with fire with this particular conversation.

"And what about foreplay?" he asked before she could formulate another question, so effortlessly turning the tables so that *she* was now sitting in the hot seat. And clearly, he liked having the upper hand.

There was no mistaking the wicked grin curving his lips, or the shameless look in his eyes that dared her to be just as bold and brazen. She'd never shied away from a little risk and adventure, and this discussion was much too entertaining to pass up.

"Well, that all depends on the situation," she said as she took another small bite of her cinnamon pastry and oh-so-slowly sucked the sweet icing off her index finger, which he watched with avid heat and interest. "I love being caressed and stroked and having a man's hands and mouth all over my body, and vice versa. I could indulge in foreplay for hours before the main act, if there's time and we both want to take it slow and tease one another."

Just the thought of Aiden's fingers and lips skimming intimate places made her pulse race a bit faster. "However, there's something to be said for a hard, fast quickie, when you're already so hot for each other that touching isn't even necessary to climax."

"Agreed," he said, the gruff, husky pitch of his voice brimming with a low, heady thrum of arousal.

She swallowed hard. He'd subtly shifted closer, his upper body now turned toward her seat. Their gazes were locked, his intense stare so hot and dark and hypnotic it seemed to singe right through her.

The sizzling arc of energy between them was palpable, and in the depth of Aiden's gaze she glimpsed all the forbidden places he could take her, the carnal pleasure he could give her, and knew an affair with a man like him would be like riding a runaway roller coaster that ended in a wild free fall.

Her stomach fluttered, the sensation spiraling south, and Chloe knew she ought to put an end to their provocative banter—they were sitting in an airplane, for God's sake—but she was much too intrigued by his responses, and very curious to know more.

"Biggest fantasy?" she asked, the question rushing past her lips in a breathy whisper before she thought better of it.

"Watching a woman pleasuring herself." His tone was soft and bone-meltingly seductive, the kind of voice she imagined he'd use when coaxing a woman to do his biding. "You?"

Chloe crossed one leg over the other, because there was a sudden throbbing, insistent ache between her thighs that was getting increasingly more difficult to ignore. "Being taken by a man. Aggressively. Passionately." A part of her was shocked that she'd truly revealed her biggest turn-on, instead of opting for a more watered down reply. But the lust reflecting in Aiden's gaze made her honesty all the more worth it.

The truth was, after her last serious relationship she had a difficult time relinquishing any kind of control, even when it came to sex. She knew her previous partners had found her intimidating in the bedroom, and she had to admit that her direct approach to sex helped to keep their affair from getting emotionally complicated. But secretly, the thought of a man being confident and aggressive enough to take charge of her pleasure was a fantasy that made her weak in the knees.

His gaze dropped to her mouth, adding to the chaotic hunger taking up residence within her. "You have icing on your bottom lip," he murmured.

The muscles in her stomach tightened, and she swiped her tongue across the plump surface, tasting the remnants of cinnamon and vanilla. He tracked the movement with his gaze and gave his head a slight shake.

"No, right *here.*" Lifting his hand, he skimmed his thumb just below the corner of her mouth, the same time she licked the exact spot.

Her tongue accidentally touched the pad of his finger, and he sucked in a harsh breath but didn't move his hand away from her face. Instead, his fingers slowly slid around to the nape of her neck and his thumb pressed gently against her jawline, holding her steady in his grasp. She watched and waited, utterly spellbound by the fascination and desire etching his gorgeous features and illuminating the brilliant blue of his eyes.

Their attraction was certainly nothing new, but this blatant hunger, well, this was exciting and potent and irresistible on so many levels. Her gaze dropped to his mouth, and her lips parted of their own accord, while her heart began a heavy, wild beat in her chest.

Had she ever wanted a kiss so badly? Not that she

could ever remember. But it was *Aiden's* kiss she craved, to the extent that nothing else mattered but feeling the heat and pressure of his mouth on hers.

He must have felt the same way, because he uttered a coarse, resigned, *"screw it,"* and gave in to the same temptation she was battling.

His lips claimed hers, as confident and persuasive as the man himself. Without preamble, his tongue slipped inside her mouth with a direct challenge, one she accepted just as eagerly. Long fingers tangled in her hair as he angled her head to the side and took her to a deeper, darker place, where two years of verbal foreplay and daring flirtations culminated into an explosive kiss that was nothing short of incendiary.

Chloe certainly felt as though she was about to go up in flames, and she moaned in the back of her throat as her body melted from all the heat they'd generated. A needful ache spiraled straight between her thighs. For all the times she'd fantasized about kissing Aiden, she had to admit that reality was far more erotic and twice as exhilarating.

With her head held in place by his big, strong hand, he controlled everything about the kiss—the rhythm, the depth, the thrust and parry of tongues—providing her with a glimpse of what a dominant lover he could be, how he'd wield that same power over her body, given the chance. The arousing thought made her purr like a cat being stroked in all the right places…until the plane hit a patch of turbulence, jarring them both back to the present.

He quickly pulled his mouth from hers and swore beneath his breath, as if belatedly realizing what he'd done and how it might affect their working relationship. She stared into his enigmatic blue eyes, just as stunned by her own reckless behavior, but she couldn't deny that his kiss had rocked her world in a major way.

She licked her bottom lip, tasting the remnants of Aiden in her mouth—a dark, delicious flavor she knew could become highly addictive, if she let it. "Why did you do that?" she asked, because he'd clearly been the one to instigate the kiss.

He withdrew his fingers from her hair and settled back into his own seat, though his gaze never left hers. "Because I have impulse control issues?" he offered as an excuse, a playful half smile curving his lips.

"Liar," she accused softly. The man was controlled at all times, and she shivered as she recalled how he'd oh-so-skillfully, and much too easily, commanded her during that intimate lip-lock.

He released a long breath and shook his head. "Honestly, it just happened. And I'd *really* be lying if I said I was sorry."

Surprisingly, she had no regrets, either. "I get it. We've been flirting with one another for the past two years, and since we're being so candid, I have to admit I've always wondered what it would be like to kiss you." Okay, she'd imagined more than just *that,* but she wasn't about to confess all the down and dirty things she'd thought about doing with him. "It's nice to know that the attraction is mutual."

"No kidding." He scrubbed a hand along his jaw and groaned. "Shit. This is bad."

"You started it," she said, and laughed, trying to make light of the situation.

He gave her an impish grin. "Yeah, and we both know it would be career suicide to see where that spontaneous kiss might take us."

It was a statement they both were very familiar with. A company edict that had served as a reminder of why there were certain personal lines they'd never crossed…until now.

"Don't worry, Aiden," she reassured him with a pat on his knee. "I don't kiss and tell, so no one at the office will ever find out."

However, having just shattered the one sacred, fundamental rule that had once stood between them, Chloe wondered how they were going to revert back to professional colleagues. Especially when their brief encounter had left her wanting much, much more.

4

Hours after arriving at the St. Raphael resort, Aiden was still wondering what the hell he'd been thinking to kiss Chloe on the plane.

The truth was, he hadn't been thinking, not with the head on his shoulders, anyways. If his brain had been functioning properly, it would have brought him to a screeching halt the moment she'd accidentally licked his finger as he'd wiped away the icing from the corner of her mouth. But years of wanting to take a bite of forbidden fruit had beckoned to him, and giving in to the temptation that was Chloe Reiss had been incredibly easy to do—especially when she'd done absolutely nothing to stop him.

That kiss had changed everything between them, because now he possessed carnal knowledge of just how sinful and decadent Chloe tasted. Now, when he glanced at her, he saw more than just an attractive business associate. Instead, he found himself looking at a hot, lush, passionate woman who made him all too aware of how long it had been since he'd indulged in steamy, mind-bending sex for nothing more than the sake of pure pleasure and satisfaction. And there was no doubt in Aiden's mind that he and Chloe had merely ignited a spark that would burn them both up in flames if one of them dared to strike that match.

Putting his attraction to Chloe out of his mind should have been easy enough to accomplish, considering they'd both shifted right into work mode after checking into the hotel. And for a few hours, anyways, he'd managed to keep his thoughts on gathering information for his campaign.

He and Chloe had spent the entire afternoon with a resort representative who'd given them a private tour of the island and amenities, and answered any questions they had about the planned curriculum. The island itself was tropical and mystical, a true paradise getaway designed for relaxation and romance. The resort's hotel was a sprawling masterpiece set along an endless white sand beach, with lagoons and waterfalls amidst a lush landscape of foliage and fragrant, exotic flowers.

They met their photographer, Ricardo, who would be taking random pictures of the resort and activities for them to use for their presentations. The man would also be on hand to do private sessions if either one of them wanted specific shots and would also provide professional models to use during the photography session.

At the end of the tour, Aiden and Chloe were given the same orientation package as all the other registrants, which included a schedule of activities, a daily itinerary and all the enhanced services the resort had to offer singles looking to make a love connection.

He'd spent the rest of the afternoon outlining a basic PowerPoint presentation based on the information he'd gleaned about the resort, as did Chloe. Tonight was the initial meet-and-greet mixer, a cocktail reception designed to kick-start the next five days of fun, sun and matchmaking events. While he needed to attend the festivities in order to evaluate the resort's quality of service and assess their current marketing strategies, Aiden wasn't looking forward to mingling with a bunch of women who were searching for a committed relationship.

Fashionably late, he walked into the large, spacious ballroom that had been set up with an elaborate buffet and an open bar. Fun reggae music native to the island played in the background for those wanting to take advantage of the dance floor.

Already, groups were forming based on the color-coded silicone wristband everyone was required to wear—a simple and effective system that let other participants know that anyone with a matching wristband was in their pool of compatible picks, based on the questionnaire they'd filled out prior to arriving on the island. Once a couple made a connection, they could then exchange their initial bracelets for matching red ones that signaled to others that they were paired off and no longer available.

First things first. He needed a drink, and he headed to the bar and ordered a Glenlivit Scotch neat. Just as he walked away, he caught sight of Chloe, surrounded by three men who wore the same bright yellow band encircling her wrist. Aiden's neon green wristband was a much needed reminder that while he and Chloe might share a hot sexual chemistry, there was the proof that they weren't compatible on other levels.

That should have been enough to put a huge damper on his desire for Chloe, but as he well knew, sometimes wanting someone had nothing to do with sharing the same ideas and values. Sometimes it was just all about pure lust and passion. And those were two things he and Chloe had in common, as they'd proved with that kiss they'd shared.

She laughed at something one of the men said, her eyes alight with amusement as she responded with a retort that had the guys chuckling, too. The spikey-haired blond dude to her left placed a possessive hand low on her back and leaned close to whisper something in her ear that made her raise a flirtatious brow.

Aiden read her lips as she said, "you're so bad," and felt a strange burning sensation in the pit of his stomach, along with the urge to join their group and stake a claim he had no right to.

He frowned to himself. Jealousy was not a feeling he was familiar with, and he wasn't happy that Chloe was the one to rouse the emotion.

Shit. He took a deep drink of his scotch, hoping the alcohol would help soothe his irritation.

"I see you're wearing a green wristband, too."

The soft, feminine voice pulled Aiden from his unpleasant thoughts and forced him to shift mental gears. Grateful for the diversion, he smiled at the petite brunette who'd approached him, noticing that her bracelet did match his. She was wearing a simple white blouse and navy blue skirt, along with a pair of flats—a very conservative choice when he compared it to the more formfitting bandage-style red dress and killer black heels Chloe had worn tonight.

This woman was plain but pretty, with kind blue eyes and a nervous smile, and he quickly tried to put her at ease.

"Hi. I'm Aiden," he said, and extended his hand toward her in greeting.

Her hand slipped into his, soft and delicate, lacking the kind of confidence he was used to in a handshake. "I'm Joy. It's nice to meet you, Aiden."

"Likewise," he replied.

She shifted anxiously on her feet, her discomfort obvious. "I'm finding this mixer so overwhelming, so I'm glad that everyone is wearing a color-coded wristband, which makes it easier to find someone who I'm compatible with, like you."

Her assumption that they were a perfect match when she didn't even know him was unnerving. Deciding she could use a bit of alcohol to loosen up, he guided her toward the bar.

"Can I get you something to drink?"

"Umm, sure." She thought for a minute. "I'll take a Roy Rogers."

He bit back a groan at her choice of mocktail—cola mixed with grenadine syrup and garnished with a maraschino cherry. He ordered her beverage, handed her the drink, and when he gravitated toward the buffet, she followed him. She was quiet and shy, and in order to fill up the awkward silence between them, he tried to keep the conversation flowing.

"So, Joy, where do you live?" he asked as he scooped some pasta salad onto his plate.

"In a small town just outside of Cincinnati, Ohio."

He was a big city kind of guy and couldn't imagine being confined to a small community. He added a chicken breast drenched in a savory sauce onto his dish, along with a warm roll and butter. "And what do you do for work?"

She selected some raw vegetables and cubes of cheese, her appetite not nearly as hearty as his own. "I'm a first grade teacher."

Interesting, and very fitting, he thought. "So you like kids?"

"I love kids." Her voice reflected her enthusiasm. "I can't wait to get married and have a big family of my own. The sooner, the better. How about you?"

She returned the question with way too much eagerness and hope in her gaze, and warning bells went off in his head. Yes, he wanted those things, too, but the way she was looking at him, as if he'd make the perfect baby daddy, sparked a bit of panic deep inside Aiden.

For the next hour, Joy stuck by his side, and he learned more about her than he ever wanted to. She loved to cook and bake, she sewed her own clothes and enjoyed gardening. She admitted to being a homebody, and had all those traditional, domestic qualities Aiden thought he wanted in a future wife.

This was the type of woman who'd been deemed a match based on the compatibility questionnaire he'd filled out, Aiden realized. On paper, she fit what he believed were non-negotiable requirements for the next woman he allowed himself to get serious with. But in reality, there was no doubt in his mind that she was way too passive and would bore the hell out of him if he had to spend more than a few hours in her company.

It was a very sobering thought.

When another guy with a green wristband started talking to Joy, Aiden used the interruption to quietly slip away and continue mingling. Unfortunately, he found himself bombarded by a steady stream of women with the same matching bracelets, and similar traits to Joy.

He smiled and nodded as the women talked and vied for his attention, but as his gaze spotted Chloe standing a few feet away, surrounded by her own male fan club, she was the one who captured his interest. He wasn't surprised to see that men with all different colored wristbands had flocked to her. Not only was she beautiful and alluring, but she was charming, intelligent and had a great sense of humor. What guy wouldn't be drawn to such a vibrant personality?

"Do you have a time frame of when you want to be married and start a family?"

The personal question from one of the women made him feel as though he was starting to suffocate, and he didn't know how much more of this charade he could take.

The problem was, he really wasn't here to find a spouse, and it wasn't fair to all these ladies to even pretend that he was. He didn't want to be continually pursued by women who believed they were a match when he had no intentions of following through, and he saw that as a potential problem as the week went on.

His reasons for being at St. Raphael were to assess the resort's current program so he could create a strong marketing campaign, and he knew he could accomplish that without all this other pretense. He had an idea in mind, and if he could get Chloe to agree, then they'd both be better able to concentrate on the business side of this trip.

Without answering the woman's question, he politely excused himself from the group and walked straight to Chloe. He came up beside her, touched her arm, and she glanced at him in surprise.

"Care to dance?" He grinned at her, hoping like hell she took pity on him.

She didn't even hesitate with her reply. "I'd love to."

He guided her toward the dance floor just as a lively reggae tune gave way to a slower melody. Stealing Chloe away earned him some serious glares from her avid suitors, but Aiden didn't care. The relief on her face told him that she appreciated the break—so maybe she wasn't cut out for this whole matchmaking scenario, either.

There were only a few other couples enjoying the music, leaving them plenty of room on the dance floor. Pulling Chloe into his embrace, Aiden tucked one of her hands in his and wrapped his other arm around her waist, bringing their bodies flush. The scent of her perfume—exotic, floral and seductive—instantly inundated his senses. She was like a femme fatale, and he desperately wanted to bury his face in her neck and inhale the intoxicating fragrance lingering on her skin.

He'd never had the pleasure of having her pressed so intimately against him, and he was instantly conscious of how perfectly her soft curves complemented his harder, masculine frame—not to mention how well the snug bodice of her dress displayed the provocative swell of her breasts.

Desire stirred deep and low, and when he met her gaze, there was no mistaking the same level of heated awareness glimmering in her hazel eyes. Absently, he stroked his palm down her spine and let his hand come to rest just above her toned bottom.

"Do you see those two men standing over there by the bar?" Chloe asked as she casually draped one of her arms around his neck.

Aiden glanced in the direction she'd indicated and frowned, something he seemed to be doing a lot of tonight when it came to her. "You mean the guys that are staring at you like hungry vultures?" He all but growled the question.

She lifted a brow, amusement glimmering in her eyes, but didn't call him on his possessive behavior. "They're staring at me because they're sizing up their competition. Those two men are from the other rival ad agency Perry told us about."

"Really?" he asked, surprised by the certainty in her voice. "How do you know that?"

"The dark-haired guy is wearing a yellow wristband like mine and he started talking to me when I first arrived," she said. "He introduced himself as Brad, and I thought he was just another single guy making the rounds. He asked me what I did for a living, so I told him I was an ad executive, and his whole demeanor changed because he must have realized who I was. He said he worked for an ad agency, too, and came right out and asked if I was here for the St. Raphael account."

Ahh, now he knew why the duo was keeping an eye on her. "I take it you told them yes?"

"I'm not going to lie about it," she said and

shrugged, seemingly unthreatened by their rival's presence. "I'd rather it be out in the open so we're sure to keep our distance."

He preferred to know who their opponent was, too, so he and Chloe could watch their backs and keep any advertising strategies to themselves. "At least now we won't be constantly wondering who the competition is."

"Exactly. I'm sure they feel the same way."

Undoubtedly. "By the way, thanks for saving me from having to deal with all those women," he said, nodding back toward were he'd left the group of ladies to dance with Chloe. They were all still clustered together—probably plotting their revenge for the way he'd abandoned them.

She followed his gaze. "They look nice enough, and they're all wearing the same colored wristband as yours. Surely you all have plenty in common based on the questionnaire you filled out."

He caught the sly smile on her lips and knew she was teasing him about their earlier conversation.

Now he had a better understanding of what she meant when she said that the survey was desperate and forced and how she preferred to let a relationship develop organically. But he still believed a quiz could help eliminate potential conflicts between two people before they invested too much time and emotion into the relationship.

He shrugged nonchalantly. "I don't know that those women and I had a lot in common, so much as their biological clocks are ticking and they're anxious to get married and have babies."

She tipped her head to the side, her body relaxing completely against his. "There must have been *something* in your answers that matched you up to those particular women. Maybe *your* biological clock is ticking?"

He smiled, as always enjoying her sense of humor. "I don't feel a sense of urgency about it, but sure, I want to get married again someday and have a family. Don't you?"

"Not anytime soon," she said with an adamant shake of her head that caused her loose hair to cascade over her bare shoulders. "I've got too many career goals I want to achieve, and that kind of focus demands all my time and energy. I'm not willing to give up my aspirations for a relationship that would demand way more than I'm willing to give."

Okay, yeah, he already knew that about Chloe. Her words reinforced once again why they were wearing different colored bracelets. "What about your lap dogs?" he teased, referring to the men who'd huddled around her, and were still watching her from across the room, waiting for an opportunity to claim her once she was free again. "Any potential suitors in the group?"

"Good Lord, no." She looked appalled by the mere suggestion. "You know I don't take all this matchmaking stuff seriously. It's fun and interesting, and I'm making mental notes for my campaign, but there will be no love match for me. I suppose I'd have a good time hanging out with a couple of those guys for the next few days, but that's about it."

That ridiculous bite of jealousy reared its ugly head again and before he could stop himself he splayed his hand at the base of her spine and pulled her lower body tighter against his. "Don't you feel bad about leading them on?"

"I'm just flirting and having fun," she said, something that was an inherent part of her personality. "I didn't say or do anything that would give any of those guys any indication that I'm interested in them on a one-on-one basis."

"Yet that's what everyone at this resort is here for," he pointed out.

"True." She sighed, a small frown creasing her brows. "I guess I'll have to be very careful about the things I say and do."

The song that was playing blended into another slow tune as more couples joined them on the dance floor. Aiden was grateful for yet another low-key ballad because he wasn't ready to let Chloe go just yet.

"Actually, I feel the same way," he said, and knew what he was about to propose would easily solve the issue, if she agreed. "I know tonight's initial meet and greet was important to both of us to see how everyone is matched up, but I'd really like to just concentrate on the business aspect of being at the resort. Since you seem to be in a similar mindset, I have a proposition to offer that would benefit both of us."

"Really?" she murmured, her eyes alight with sensual interest as her fingers threaded through the hair at the nape of his neck. "You have my undivided attention."

Her tone was ripe with innuendo. Clearly, Chloe's mind had gone the playful, naughty route, enticing a grin from him. "It's nothing indecent."

She feigned a guileless pout. "Too bad."

Chloe had always been a shameless flirt and a tease, but after that kiss, everything between them now smoldered with an underlying heat and hunger. He was keenly aware of everything about her, making it impossible to ignore the erotic slide of her thighs against his, the heady scent lingering on her skin, and the delectable lips he wanted to taste again.

Hell, who did he think he was kidding? The impulse to claim her mouth for another deep, drugging kiss was just the tip of the iceberg. He had a list of all sorts of wicked things he wanted to do to her, with her. But mostly, he wanted to be that man to tap into her secret fantasy, to assert a bit of aggression and coax her to completely surrender to the darker side of pleasure.

"So, what's this proposition of yours?" she asked curiously.

He exhaled a deep breath, which did absolutely nothing to lessen the sexual tension coursing through his body. He was certain nothing short of a cold shower would help at this point. "Since neither one of us is interested in being pursued this week, what do you think about trading in our current wristbands for matching red ones?"

She raised a perfectly arched brow as she contemplated his suggestion. "You want us to be a couple?"

"In wristband only," he clarified, though the longer he remained pressed up against her, the more his unruly body clamored for the real deal. "If we're both wearing a red bracelet, which lets everyone know that we've found a match and are no longer interested in mingling, then we can give one hundred percent of our attention to what we need to do for our respective presentations. We can attend events together, or separately, without having to worry about other people thinking we're still single."

"That's a great idea," she said enthusiastically. "It'll eliminate the problem of having to turn down overtures from men I really have no interest in."

"Then let's do it."

"Right now?" She widened her eyes in scandalized shock as she deliberately chose to put a playful, suggestive twist on his words. "Here? In front of everyone?"

He chuckled. "Yeah, what can I say. Beneath this stuffy suit and tie, I'm really an exhibitionist."

"Hmm. You and I might be compatible after all." Her gaze sparkled with laughter. "Now let's go switch out these wristbands."

5

CHLOE MET AIDEN for a late morning brunch in the dining room, where they enjoyed an elaborate spread of food ranging from health-conscious dishes to rich, gourmet cuisine. There was something for everyone, and so far she was impressed with the resort's selection of meal options, and the service, too.

She finished off her banana fosters crepe, and the efficient waitstaff promptly cleared her plate and refilled her cup with fresh, steaming coffee before she could even ask. She stirred cream and sugar into the brew and glanced across the table at Aiden, who'd just taken the last bite of his fully loaded omelet.

Today they were wearing matching red wristbands, indicating they were a couple, and so far, the ruse was working. None of the other singles approached them, which allowed both her and Aiden to just relax and do what they'd come to St. Raphael to accomplish.

"What are you in the mood to do today?" she asked him.

A wicked grin tipped up one corner of his mouth. "Is that a trick question?"

No, it wasn't, but after that heated kiss on the plane and feeling his hard, masculine body moving rhythmically against hers as they'd danced last night, she could think of a dozen different things she'd rather do with him than the various ice-breaker activities the resort had to offer. But those more erotic, get-naked-and-burn-up-the-sheets-together type games weren't an option for them, despite how much she wished otherwise.

"I was talking about what's on the list of organized activities scheduled for the afternoon and evening," she said, passing him the single sheet of paper listing the day's events. "Is there anything in particular you'd like to check out?"

He leaned back in his chair and looked over their options. "There's certainly a lot to choose from."

She agreed. The activity director had covered the gamut of recreational offerings, from the basic getting-to-know-you trivia contests to the more lively, physically interactive games for those who enjoyed a bit more adventure and uninhibited fun. Each event was rated from mild to wild, so there was no confusing the level of sexual content in each activity.

Aiden glanced at his wristwatch. "Looks like there's a golf tournament starting in half an hour."

She rolled her eyes and shook her head. "Forget about it. Golf is one of the most boring sports *ever.*"

"How about the wet and wild T-shirt competition?" he suggested, and waggled his brows at her way too lasciviously.

He was such a *guy.* "Only if you'll agree to learn the cha-cha with me," she replied just as audaciously.

He visibly cringed at her suggestion, though the laughter in his eyes gave him away. "Okay, I guess *neither* of those things will be happening."

There were a few activities on the list that no longer applied to them since they were now a couple. There was no need for the speed dating event, or any of the other singles mixers, so Chloe figured they might as well choose something fun and entertaining.

After taking a sip of her coffee, she tossed out the one idea that appealed to her the most. "I was thinking that the risqué charades could be kind of amusing to watch, but that's not for another two hours."

"That would give us some time to walk around the resort and check things out now that everything is in full swing."

She nodded. "That's a good idea. I also want to talk to Ricardo about setting up a time frame tomorrow for him to take certain pictures for my presentation."

"I need to do the same thing." He placed his napkin on his empty plate and stood, looking extremely handsome in a casual gray polo and khaki cargo shorts. The man pulled off the executive look as well as a more casual style with equal aplomb. "Shall we?"

She joined him, and together they walked out of the hotel to the pool and lounge area. The sun was shining, making it a beautiful, cloudless day, perfect for outdoor activities. The area was quickly filling up with singles and couples, and laughter rang out as a nearby drinking game at the underground pool bar turned a bit rowdy. Other men and women were heading down a pathway that led to the beach to enjoy a swim in the ocean, or participate in the ongoing volleyball game on the sand.

Waiters carrying trays of fruity rum drinks aptly named "Love Potion" seemed to be everywhere. Chloe grabbed one for herself and Aiden as they watched a Ping-Pong tournament for a while before moving on to the game of bikini Twister that had them at times cringing and chuckling out loud as nearly naked, oil-slicked bodies vied for space on the overly large Twister mat. Each turn of the spinner had the men and women switching into very interesting and compromising positions that Chloe couldn't imagine executing in a public place.

"I'd love to see the greenhouse they have here on the island," Chloe said, ready for something a bit more low-key and quiet. "Want to join me?"

He gave a nonchalant shrug. "Sure. We still have a little bit of time to kill before charades."

Chloe swapped out her empty glass for a refill of the fruity cocktail, then followed the signs pointing the way toward the botanical garden. The sounds of calypso music faded the farther away they walked from the hotel, while the lush green foliage and bright flowers and shrubbery increased. Most of the plants along the way were labeled with their name, origin and description. The intoxicating scent of jasmine hung in the air, seductive and alluring… as if pulling Chloe toward a magical place.

She sipped on her drink as the narrow pathway eventually gave way to a smaller, more intimate area, with a gazebo and greenhouse filled with beautiful, vivid flowers. Intrigued, Chloe gravitated toward the glass-enclosed nursery, and Aiden followed. As soon as they stepped inside, they were wrapped in humidity and the perfumed scent of flowers.

With no one else around, it was quiet and peaceful, and stunningly beautiful. Chloe wasn't one to stop and smell the roses, so to speak, but she was completely in awe of all the beauty surrounding her. She and Aiden walked along the rows of floral displays, taking in the dozens of exotic blooms in brilliant hues, and more species of orchids than she realized existed—all labeled with names and descriptions.

Drawn to a unique cluster of fuchsia flowers that looked like a cross between a lily and an orchid, she studied the blossoms, fascinated by the way the inside folds looked similar to a woman's vulva, with a small nub resembling a clitoris, while the thick stamen gave the impression of a very large, erect penis.

"This one looks like a combination of female and male genitalia," she murmured in amusement, her thoughts tumbling out of her mouth thanks to the alcohol loosening her tongue.

Aiden moved closer to get a better look, the warmth of his body and the brush of his arm against hers causing her nipples to tighten in awareness. Everything inside this greenhouse—the steamy humidity, the drugging scent in the air, the erotic flowers—made her think of sex.

"The flower definitely has a lot of similarities," he agreed, his voice low and huskier than normal, as if he, too, was affected by the sensual atmosphere.

Drawn to the bright pink flower, Chloe reached out to caress the protruding yellow stamen—even though she knew better than to touch something so fragile.

"Hello, you two," a soft female voice said from behind them, causing Chloe to snap out of her weird trance and snatch her hand back before she could make contact with the fuzzy stalk.

Startled by the fact that they weren't alone as she'd originally thought, both she and Aiden turned around to face the person who'd spoken—an older woman, probably in her sixties, with dark brown skin, warm brown eyes and a kind, welcoming smile. She was wearing a colorful caftan dress with billowing sleeves and her hair was wrapped atop her head in multiple braids entwined with colorful strips of fabric.

"We didn't realize someone else was here," Aiden said.

"I'm the greenhouse caretaker," the other woman explained, spreading her arms wide to encompass the area, her voice filled with pride. "My name is Hattie, but here on the island, they call me the matchmaker."

"To tie in to the theme here at the resort?" Chloe guessed, curious to know the woman's angle.

Something mystical twinkled in the older woman's eyes. "Some would say so, but while the resort has managed to find a way to modernize a love connection between two people, I still prefer to do things the old-fashioned way."

Chloe wasn't sure what the woman meant by that, but before she or Aiden could ask, Hattie spoke once again.

"It's nice to have some visitors. With the resort offering so many activities, not many travel down this path to the greenhouse," she said, her gaze seemingly scrutinizing the two of them with a discerning amount of insight. "Usually just the couples with a romantic soul."

Chloe resisted the urge to roll her eyes. She didn't want to offend the woman. But she couldn't help but wonder if Hattie was feeding them a line, to make it seem as though the greenhouse possessed some sort of mysterious, enchanting properties. Then again, hadn't Chloe just been mesmerized by that erotic flower she'd nearly touched?

Hattie glanced at the matching red bands on their wrists, a knowing smile curving the corner of her lips. "I love seeing when two people find their soul mate early on in the week."

Realizing that the woman thought she and Aiden were a real couple, Chloe shook her head. "Oh, we're not together that way," she quickly clarified. "The bracelets are just a distraction. We're one of the ad agencies here to work on a marketing campaign for the resort. This is just a pretense so we don't have to mingle like everyone else."

Hattie moved to a row of plants on a long table and tested the soil with her fingers before plucking away a few wilting leaves. "Trust me, the two of you were meant for one another."

Hattie's statement couldn't have been further from the truth, but there was a calm certainty in her voice that made Chloe's heart skip a weird beat.

Aiden shifted besides Chloe. "How do you know that the two of us are…uh, soul mates?" he asked.

Chloe frowned at him and his question. Had he really gotten sucked into the woman's claim that she had the ability to predict a couple's compatibility? The man was far more intelligent than that, but he appeared truly interested in the woman's reply.

"The easiest answer is your pheromones," she said with a shrug. "I can't give away all my secrets, but I come from a very long line of matchmakers, and I'm rarely, if ever, wrong about my predictions."

"So, when couples happen into your greenhouse, you can just sense their compatibility?" he asked, a skeptical note in his voice.

"Yes, I just know," she said with the conviction of a woman who was confident in her abilities. "But everyone always seems to want some sort of tangible proof in order to believe my claim. This very unique hybrid flower, which is native to this island, provides that." She indicated the bright pink flower that Chloe had nearly touched. "I call it the flower of love. I like to think it represents love and passion, because that's the results it produces."

"What does it do?" Chloe asked, curious despite her very practical nature.

Hattie smiled. "When a couple touches the stamen at the same time, it changes color. Sometimes it's two different colors, which indicates incompatibility. But when the color is the same, well, that's when the true magic of love happens. Would the two of you like to give it a try?"

Chloe's heart was suddenly beating hard and fast in her chest, and she wasn't sure why. She was torn between wanting to scoff at such nonsense, yet she was tempted to see how the whole color-change thing worked. And did she really want to know the results she and Aiden produced?

Aiden made the decision for them. "What the hell," he said unexpectedly. "Let's do it."

Alrighty then. Chloe exhaled a deep breath, and reached toward the flower the same time that Aiden did. With her thumb and forefinger, she lightly grasped the stamen, right below where Aiden touched. Beneath the pad of their fingers, a deep, dark purple hue saturated the delicate stalk.

"Ahhh," Hattie said, her voice infused with satisfaction and excitement. "Desire, lust and love. I was right. The two of you are extremely compatible."

Chloe quickly pulled her hand back, while Aidan did so more casually. She couldn't dispute the desire simmering between them, but the other emotion Hattie spoke of, well, that she *could* argue. "We're not in love."

Hattie tipped her head to the side, her brown eyes gentle yet insistent. "But you have the potential to be, if you open yourselves up to it."

AS THEY WALKED back to the resort a few minutes later, Chloe cast a glance at Aiden, who'd been oddly quiet since the older woman's spiel. "So, what do you think of Hattie the Matchmaker and her claims?"

"Do I believe she just knows that two people belong together, with or without that flower trick?" He shook his head, clearly a man who thought in pragmatic terms. "No, I don't. However, I think I just found my marketing angle for my campaign."

"Really?" No wonder Aiden had asked so many questions, and had so willingly gone along with all of Hattie's antics. "So, you're going to spin the fact that St. Raphael has an actual, old-fashioned match-maker on the island?"

"Absolutely." He gave her a smug smile. "And I'm going to make it work in a way that's going to increase the resort's exposure and gives them an added edge over their competition." He grabbed her hand and picked up their pace along the walkway. "Come on, we need to hustle or we're going to be late for the risqué charades."

Liking the feel of her hand enclosed in his, Chloe tried not to read too much into the gesture, though it did make her feel a little warm and mushy inside. Or maybe that light, pleasant buzz she was experiencing was a result of that second love potion drink. As she looked at Aiden's face, she could see that his mental gears were already churning out ideas for his presentation, and she had to admit that using Hattie and her traditional methods of matchmaking, beyond standard compatibility quizzes, would provide a unique twist to Aiden's campaign.

He'd just verbally staked a claim to Hattie and her matchmaking knowledge—which they've done plenty of times in the past to make sure the other person didn't latch on to the same idea, too. Now Chloe just had to find a bigger and better hook for her own presentation. She had something in mind, but wasn't quite ready to share her concept just yet.

Back inside the hotel, they entered the room for the charades just as the men and women were in the process of dividing into teams. Chloe intended to sit on the sidelines and just enjoy the show, but when one of the teams came up short a couple, she and Aiden were recruited to play. With a little alcohol in her system, it didn't take long for her to put the incident at the greenhouse out of her mind, loosen up and get into the spirit of the game…and the competition.

Each couple drew a phrase from a large glass bowl, and a timer was set for three minutes. Back and forth the teams battled for supremacy, playacting the expression or sentence they'd been given, which ranged from a couple having sex on a sandy beach, skinny dipping in the ocean, impatient newlyweds on their wedding night, to a couple playing nurse and doctor.

More rum cocktails were served, and inhibitions were shed as everyone got into character to execute their scenes. The sketches were at times bawdy and X-rated, and hilarious to watch unfold as different guesses were shouted out. Chloe's sides ached from so much laughter.

She and Aiden managed to avoid being chosen until the very end of the game, when it came down to a win-or-lose tiebreaker for their group. Since they were the only couple who hadn't performed, it was up to them to score the last point in order for their team to win.

"Bring it on!" someone on their team cheered as Chloe and Aiden stepped up to the small staging area.

Chloe flashed Aiden a sassy smile. "You know I

don't like to lose at anything, so you'd better bring your A-game."

"You're such an overachiever," he teased as he reached into the glass bowl and randomly withdrew one of the crumpled pieces of paper.

She rubbed her hands together. "Failure is not an option for me."

He unfolded the paper, silently read their phrase and grinned like a tempting rogue. "Are you sure you're ready for this?"

Judging by the sinful look on his face, Chloe was certain he'd selected one of the more daring expressions—but then again, this *was* risqué charades so she'd expected something outrageous. "You know I love a good challenge."

"Well, then, here you go." He revealed the act they had to execute.

Making out in the backseat of a car.

Getting their team to guess "backseat of a car" was a fairly easy process and took less than thirty seconds of their time. After that Chloe and Aiden embraced in order to playact the first part of the parody. Their bodies entwined and Aiden ran his flattened palms up and down her back while she threaded her fingers through his hair in an attempt to look like frenzied teenagers in the throes of passion. The only thing *not* touching were their lips. Chloe was pretty certain that Aiden was trying to avoid a repeat performance of yesterday's kiss.

Unfortunately, everyone on their team shouted out

words that were close to the phrase, but not an exact match. There was groping, feeling up, hugging and heavy petting, but no "making out."

"You have one minute left," someone yelled.

With time running out, and the lingering effects of the love potion drink coursing through Chloe's system and bolstering her courage, she decided to give their onlookers the real deal. No way was she going to let them lose this one last point because she hadn't given all she had to beat the competition. Not if she could help it.

Sliding her fingers around to the back of Aiden's head, she pulled his mouth down to hers. The moment their lips touched, everything around Chloe faded away, except for her desire for this man who tempted her like no other. There was no hesitation on his part, either, just a mutual hunger that promised all sorts of wanton pleasure.

Despite having an audience, there was nothing sweet or chaste about this kiss. With a rumbling groan she felt, more than heard from Aiden, his tongue touched and tangled with hers, sweeping deep inside her mouth to dominate and possess. His hands got into the action, too, skimming along the outside of her thighs and grabbing her ass to simulate the phrase that no one had guessed yet.

Excitement sent Chloe's pulse racing and had her body melting into a pool of lust and need. Kissing Aiden was akin to the most delicious kind of foreplay, providing a hot tease of what other carnal delights his mouth and tongue were capable of giving.

Lost in pure unadulterated sensation, she was having a difficult time remembering that they were playing charades, that this was all pretend for the sake of a game. Her attraction to Aiden was real and undeniable, and in that wild moment of abandon, she wasn't sure she wanted to resist him any longer.

Her decision was absolute craziness, she knew. The risks involved were enormous, but being here on this secluded island, where no one knew who they were, was to their benefit, as well. Far away from work, prying eyes, and rules and restrictions, they had the perfect opportunity to finally indulge in what they both wanted—each other—without the worry of being caught. A quickie affair to diminish all the sexual tension burning between them. They could return to Boston and the firm with a clear head, completely focused on their respective campaigns.

Outside of her current sensual universe, she heard cheers and catcalls because of their avid embrace, and finally, through all the commotion, someone shouted out the correct phrase, "making out in the backseat of a car," giving their team the last point they needed to win the entire game.

She pulled back and ended the kiss, and for a long moment they stared at one another, breathless and aroused, while their team celebrated their success around them.

"I'm beginning to think that maybe you really

are an exhibitionist," she said, referring to the comment he'd made to her last night on the dance floor. "You quite enjoyed that kiss and certainly didn't hold back."

He didn't deny her allegation as he slowly released her, so that their bodies were no longer intimately entangled. "I'll admit, you have a good game strategy, Reiss."

She flashed him a daring grin full of sass. "Who said that kiss was a game?"

With that, she walked away from him. She could feel Aiden staring after her, pondering her parting remark, and knew she'd just given him a whole lot to think about—which is exactly what she'd intended. Because tonight, at dinner, she was going to turn up the heat and let him decide if he was interested in taking the bait.

6

AIDEN ESCORTED CHLOE toward the large ballroom hosting one of tonight's dining options, excruciatingly aware of her, in every way. It wasn't so much what she was wearing, though the chocolate-brown dress definitely drew his attention. The top portion fell off of one shoulder, revealing an alluring expanse of creamy skin, and the fitted skirt showcased her toned ass and ended just above her knee, accentuating her long, slender legs. Her four-inch heels were the strappy kind that wrapped around her ankles and screamed *fuck me, please.*

The thought of doing just that made him hot and hard.

She'd worn her hair piled up on her head, giving her a slightly tousled look and exposed the elegant line of her throat. An assortment of gold bangles encircled her wrist and a pair of shiny gold hoops dangled from her ears. Her green-gold eyes were full of mystery, like a siren experienced in luring a man to commit all sorts of carnal sins.

But what was making it difficult to function was the air of confidence she moved with. It made him wonder what she was up to, though he definitely had a clue. Especially after the subtle challenge she'd issued that afternoon that had him seriously considering crossing some very strict personal and professional boundaries with her.

Normally, he wrestled with his conscience when it came to wanting Chloe, but right now the only voice in his head was his brother Sam's, telling Aiden to stop overanalyzing things, that giving in to his desire for Chloe was all about feel-good sex, not a lifetime commitment.

Maybe, just maybe, for once his brother was right.

Tonight, they'd been given the choice between attending a Murder Mystery Fete, or a Truth or Dare Soiree—both events had been designed to create more social interaction between couples and singles. Since neither one of them were mystery buffs, they'd both decided on the latter, and as they stepped into a ballroom decorated in red and black tones, with sheer draping and candles flickering everywhere, a bubbly hostess greeted them.

"Welcome to the Truth or Dare Soiree. I see the two of you are a couple," the young woman said as she glanced at their matching red wristbands. "That gives you two options tonight. Would you like a group table to share with other couples, or a private table for two?"

Aiden knew there was security in large numbers, which the group table would provide, but he didn't want to go the safe route with Chloe tonight. Between all the sexual tension that had thrummed between them in the greenhouse, and later at the risqué charades, he was more than ready to kick things between them up a notch or two.

"We'll take one of the private tables."

The approving smile that Chloe gave Aiden told him he'd made the right decision. They followed the hostess to one of the secluded tables at the back of the room. Instead of taking the chair across from Chloe, he settled into the seat next to hers. Beneath the table, their thighs brushed, and neither one of them moved or shied away from the intimate contact.

"Here is a list of meal options," the hostess said, handing them each a menu before she indicated a tray with a few items on it. "As for the truth-or-dare part of tonight's dinner, it's a very simple game that will require you both to answer a truth, or accept a dare, depending on what the roll of the die reveals."

On the tray was a red cube stamped with the words *Truth* and *Dare* on each of the six sides. Next to that were four tall silver cylinders holding long wooden sticks. Each cylinder was marked TRUTH or DARE, along with the "mild" or "wild" option in each category.

"Once you roll the die, your partner will pick one

of the wooden sticks from the corresponding container," the hostess went on to explain. "They will then read aloud the truth or dare printed on the stick, and the other person must either answer the question or complete the task. Most important, have fun!"

"Thank you," Chloe said, and picked up her menu to peruse the meal options.

Aiden followed her lead, and when the waiter arrived at their table, he ordered the rib-eye steak and potatoes, and Chloe opted for the grilled salmon and rice pilaf. When they were offered either wine or champagne, he went for the cabernet, while Chloe asked for an iced tea, citing that she'd consumed way too many love potions cocktails that afternoon.

Once the waiter was gone and they were alone again, Chloe eyed the red die on the tray, a very vixenlike smile curving her mouth. "So, shall we play?" she asked him.

He took a drink of his cabernet and quirked a brow at her. "Are you sure you want to?"

She leaned a bit closer, amusement shimmering in her gaze. "What, are you afraid of having to give up deep, dark secrets?"

"I have no problem sharing truths," he replied. The loose top portion of her dress slipped a bit lower on her arm, distracting him a moment with the urge to trail his fingers along that smooth, tanned skin, all the way up to the side of her neck. "I'm just thinking of what dares might be in store for us."

"I can handle *any* dare thrown my way," she said boldly. "How about you?"

"Oh, absolutely." He waved a hand toward the game items. "By all means, ladies first."

She rolled the single red die, and the word *Truth* remained faceup. Deciding to go easy on Chloe for the first round, Aiden selected a wooden stick from the "mild" category.

He read the question out loud. "What is the reason why your last *serious* relationship ended?" Recalling their vague conversation on the plane about the guy she'd been dating, he acted on a hunch. "And I don't think that guy I saw you with at the Executive Bar counts."

Her body language stiffened slightly, enough to tell Aiden that she'd been about to go the easy and superficial route with her reply. "Why not?"

He met her gaze and held it directly, not at all put off by the defensive tone of her voice. "Because I get the impression that he was more of a temporary thing, than someone you'd been committed to."

She glanced away, and when she hesitated, he knew he'd assumed correctly. She absently bit the corner of her lip and he was struck at how vulnerable she looked in that moment, an emotion he never would have equated with the strong, always self-assured Chloe, had he not witnessed it himself.

Clearly, she didn't want to discuss her last serious relationship. But Aiden was suddenly intrigued and wanted to find out what had happened that had made her so guarded, and how her past experience had shaped her current views on relationships, as his own divorce had.

"Spill the truth, Reiss," he said, adding just enough of a challenge to his voice that he knew she'd never back down from. "That's the name of this game."

Schooling her features into an indifferent expression, she shrugged her bared shoulder. "I broke up with Neil because he was a real asshole."

Aiden smirked. Okay, that was succinct, he thought, more curious than ever. But being an asshole translated to many things, and she'd just avoided the truth of the matter with a vague reply. "You're cheating," he murmured as he swirled his red wine in his glass. "And I've never pegged you for someone who would skirt any issue."

That bit of prompting made her chin jut out stubbornly, and he waited patiently to see which direction she decided to take this conversation—avoid it completely, or give him a glimpse of something personal, and clearly, painful for her.

"Obviously, Neil isn't someone I like to talk about. If I could, I'd erase the eighteen months we were together." She paused, as if deciding what she wanted to reveal, then spoke again. "I met him my junior year in college, and everything was fine our first year together, until we got engaged, and then he… changed."

Aiden was very familiar with how people could

change, how someone *he'd* trusted so implicitly could betray him so completely and leave him with devastating regrets that would haunt him for the rest of his life. He never, ever, wanted to be blindsided like that again.

So yeah, he understood that kind of deception, and was surprised that he and Chloe shared a very similar past. The revelation was unexpected, and made him feel a strange, emotional bond with her.

The waiter came by with their dinner salads, and once he was gone Aiden returned to their conversation. "How did he change?" he asked gently.

"At first, it was all very subtle and I didn't even realize what he was doing," she said as she pushed her lettuce leaves around on her plate before taking a small bite. "But little by little, he started controlling every aspect of my life. Since we were engaged, it seemed logical to me that we open joint checking and savings accounts together. He monitored everything, which I didn't have a problem with until he started criticizing me for spending even a penny more over *his* budget, even if it was basic necessities that I needed. Yet he never had to account for anything. He obsessively checked my texts and emails, and accused me of sneaking around on him when he had no evidence. He caused problems at the ad agency where I was working, and alienated all my friends so I had no one left but him."

The pain in Chloe's gaze spoke volumes. "Neil also developed an explosive temper I'd never seen before. He was so certain I was having an affair with one of the guys at the office, that one night when I stayed late with Simon to finish up a campaign for the next day, Neil came to the office and physically assaulted the poor guy in front of my coworkers. A few days later, I was conveniently laid off."

Her mouth flattened into a thin, bitter line. "In short, he turned into an asshole. And I was so gullible and stupid I didn't even see it coming until after he cost me my job at the agency."

Instinctively, Aiden reached out and placed his hand over hers, giving it a comforting squeeze. "That doesn't make you stupid, Chloe. Just trusting."

"No, *stupid,*" she reiterated adamantly. "My mother has a history of hooking up with these same types of men, the kind that charm their way in, then take over everything. I saw it growing up, over and over again, and I swore I'd never let any man have that much control over my life... It's kind of ironic though, the first guy I get really serious about ends up being a jerk who could have been handpicked by my mother."

Finished with his salad, Aiden pushed his dish aside. "Where has your dad been in all this?"

A hint of sadness passed over her features. "He died in a motorcycle accident before I was born. I never had the chance to know him."

"I'm sorry," Aiden said, blown away by everything she'd just shared. "At least you found out about

Neil's tendencies before you married him." Aiden hadn't been that fortunate.

She stared at him as the waiter cleared their salad plates and set down their dinner dishes. Her expression turned contemplating, and he knew she was analyzing him now that she'd just laid herself bare emotionally.

"Why did you get divorced?" she asked as she picked up a piece of her salmon with her fork.

He took a bite of his steak. His rib eye was just the way he liked it—seared on the outside and medium rare inside. While he appreciated that Chloe had played the game fairly and had answered her question honestly, he didn't want to add his own depressing story about his marriage and divorce to tonight's conversation. And luckily, he had a legitimate excuse not to.

"I plead the fifth," he said, and grinned at her. "The question about serious relationships was *yours* to answer, not mine."

She wrinkled her cute little nose at him. "You suck, Landry."

A teasing glimmer returned to her eyes and he chuckled. "Yeah, I do suck," he said, purposely using the playful innuendo to lighten up their exchange. "Are you sure you want to have *that* discussion?"

"I'm sure it would be a far more enjoyable conversation than the one we just had," she grumbled beneath her breath.

So, she was still holding a little bit of a grudge

that she'd gotten the short end of the stick—so to speak—even though the very personal question had been selected randomly. "Isn't that what this matchmaking resort, and these games we're playing, are all about?" he asked, looking at the experience as the advertising executive he was. "Meeting someone you're compatible with and having deep, meaningful discussions that dig deeper than all that superficial stuff that doesn't matter when it comes to developing a long-term relationship?"

She arched a brow and pointed her fork at him. "If you'll remember correctly, we weren't originally wearing matching wristbands. So technically, you and I aren't compatible, no matter what Hattie and that silly flower indicated today. So it really wasn't necessary for me to give you all the details of my dysfunctional past with Neil, and my mother."

He couldn't argue her point, but he didn't regret pulling that particular question, or hearing her answer. Listening to her story gave him a whole new perspective on her strong-willed personality. Beneath her driven and focused attitude was a woman who'd been emotionally manipulated by a man she'd trusted, and now she channeled all her energy and passion into the one thing she could control—her career.

Yes, he now had a greater understanding of where her motivation to succeed came from, but it didn't change the fact that her single-minded determination, to the exclusion of everything else in her life, made Chloe the exact kind of woman he'd never get involved with on an emotional level.

His physical attraction to her, however, was beginning to be a whole different issue.

"I know we probably have different views on fundamental and personal matters," he said as he cut off another slice of steak, "but that hot kiss on the plane, and again this afternoon during charades, is more than enough proof that we'd be a perfect match in other ways."

A sensual, knowing smile tipped up her lips. "Well, sexual chemistry wears off, and then you're left with everything that doesn't work in a long-term relationship."

He held her gaze, deliberate and direct with his reply. "Who said anything about long-term?"

Her eyes widened ever so slightly, a little bit shocked at his blatant overture. Yeah, he went there. Put into words what they'd both been sidestepping since the day they'd started working together at Perry & Associates. He wasn't alone in this attraction, and being on this secluded tropical island, their desire for one another was at an all-time high, making the situation ripe for a hot, no-holds-barred tryst.

He'd just issued a subtle invitation, but by the end of the evening there would be no doubt in Chloe's mind exactly what he wanted—a steamy, lust-fueled night of sex with her.

With that decision made, he picked up the die and rolled for his turn. The word *Truth* remained faceup and he watched a slow, tempting smile curve the corners of her mouth. He was certain things were about to get very interesting, since *she'd* be selecting one of the wooden sticks.

Would she keep things modest as he had, or go for something more extreme?

CHLOE LOOKED FROM Aiden to the game containers on the table, quietly contemplating which category she'd choose—mild or wild. Her mind was still reeling after the very personal discussion they'd had...all because Aiden had picked a more reserved question. Considering she was still dealing with the churning in the pit of her stomach that always accompanied thoughts of her relationship with Neil, Chloe was ready to go the spontaneous and fun route to alleviate the tension of everything she'd just revealed to Aiden.

Besides, his insinuation of an affair had completely changed the tone of the game and gave the atmosphere between them a seductive vibe, and that was definitely the path in which she wanted to continue this soiree.

She waited a few seconds while their waiter whisked away their finished dinner plates, then selected a wooden stick from the wild container. She felt her face flame as she silently read the very risqué question, and knew that Aiden was definitely going to enjoy answering this one.

"If I was a type of fruit, what would I be and how would you eat me?"

Pure, unadulterated *wickedness* was the only word to describe the grin on Aiden's lips. "That's easy. You'd be a ripe, juicy peach," he said in a low, throaty sound that hypnotized her. "And you'd be so good to eat. I'd open you up with my thumbs and catch all that sweet nectar on my tongue, and suck gently on the soft center of your core until my entire mouth is filled with the taste of you."

Holy crap. The look in his eyes was so freakin' hot, and combined with that erotic description of him eating her as a peach, well, she felt breathless and thoroughly aroused. Beneath the table, she crossed her legs as a steady, throbbing sensation settled between her thighs, but the pressure only increased that agonizing need he'd just inflicted upon her. To be touched, stroked, sucked…

"Your turn," he said, as if he hadn't just filled her mind with such provocative, unforgettable, erotic images.

She reached for the die and gave it a light toss across the table. The first *Dare* presented itself, and Aiden didn't hesitate in plucking one of the sticks from the wild category. Chloe swallowed hard and prepared herself for an outrageous challenge.

Aiden smirked as he divulged the adventure he'd selected for her. "Pick up a stemmed Maraschino cherry with your lips. Feed the cherry to your partner using only your mouth, then tie the cherry stem using only your tongue. No hands allowed."

"No problem," she said, prepared to dazzle Aiden with her skills in tying a cherry stem with her tongue. Who would have thought that a silly talent she'd perfected as a teenager would come in handy one day?

He motioned to their waiter and asked for a few stemmed cherries. While the other man headed off in the direction of the bar, Chloe glanced around at all the other nearby tables. Everyone was having fun playing the truth-or-dare game. The groups of singles were laughing and cheering their teammates on, and the couples who sat alone like her and Aiden were either engrossed in a truthful conversation, or doing equally intimate dares with their partners.

The waiter returned and set a small plate with three Maraschino cherries in the middle of the table, and at the same time delivered their desserts—a slice of cheesecake drizzled with a rich-looking caramel sauce. Chloe was tempted to take a bite, but not until she finished executing her dare.

Folding her hands securely in her lap, she glanced from the dish, to Aiden. "Since I can't use my hands, you'll have to feed me one of the cherries to get me started."

More than happy to accommodate her, he picked up a cherry by the stem and dropped it into her waiting mouth. First, she had to transfer the actual cherry to Aiden, and in order to do so she needed his lips on hers.

Tucking the piece of fruit against the inside of her cheek, she crooked a beckoning finger at him. "Come closer," she cajoled sweetly, and when he did as she asked, she framed his face in her hands and brought his mouth to hers. "The cherry is for you, but first, you'll have to find it."

She could have kept things chaste and pushed the cherry immediately into his mouth, but this evening wasn't about playing it safe. Not any longer. She kissed him, her lips parting to invite him inside. His tongue glided along hers as they played hide-and-seek with the piece of fruit and she let him chase the treat until she was ready to end the playfully hot kiss. Finally, his tongue curled around the cherry and he drew it into his mouth. She clamped down on the end of the stem between her teeth, allowing him to bite off the Maraschino to enjoy.

While she went to work on the second part of her task, he chewed and swallowed the cherry, then grinned like a rogue. "Not quite as good as eating a peach," he said meaningfully.

Oh, he was so bad. A slow burn blossomed in her belly, and spread lower...to the exact part of her he associated with a ripe, juicy peach. With seductive eyes, he continued watching her as she manipulated the stem with her teeth, lips and tongue. Less than a minute later, she presented him with the cherry stem, now with a tight knot in the middle.

"Voila!" she said, proud of her accomplishment.

Amusement etched his gorgeous features. “Very impressive.”

She laughed huskily and gave him something else to consider and mentally fantasize about. “My tongue is quite talented and can do all kinds of neat tricks.”

“I’ll just bet it can,” he murmured, and rolled the die she’d nudged toward him since it was his turn, which landed on another *Dare.*

Feeling bolder and more brazen with each scene they completed, she went straight for a wild adventure. Anticipation spread throughout her entire body as she read his challenge. “Suck on your partner’s finger for one full minute.”

With a slow, shameless smile that ramped up her awareness of what he was about to do, he gently grabbed her wrist and pulled her hand toward him…and unexpectedly dragged the tip of her finger through the sticky caramel sauce on his dessert plate. The impulsive move startled her, but not as much as the wet heat of his mouth as he gradually pulled her index finger all…the…way…in.

Her breath hitched in her throat, then released in a low, sensual moan as he leisurely sucked the caramel off her finger, his gaze so dark and smoldering she knew what it was like to melt from the inside out. His tongue was as soft as velvet along her skin, and the scrape of his teeth added a sharp, erotic edge of pleasure that made her shift in her chair. With excruciating thoroughness, he licked his way all the way to the tip, then drew the digit deep once again.

Her eyes rolled back, and she bit her bottom lip to hold in another groan. She felt that suctioning pull on her nipples, which peaked into tight, hard pebbles against her top. And when he flicked his tongue along the sensitive skin between her fingers, it was as though he somehow had a direct link to her sex and had just stroked his tongue deep between the moist folds of flesh between her thighs. She had the vague thought that if he kept this up, she was going to end up climbing onto his lap right here and now and demand satisfaction.

Abruptly, he stopped and let go of her hand, jarring her back to reality and the fact that they were in a room full of people. But the hungry look in his eyes told her that he was just as affected as she was. The air between them was fueled with sexual tension, and she needed an orgasm so badly, she was close to begging for it.

Finished playing it safe, she decided to do exactly that. "Aiden—"

He pressed two fingers against her lips and shook his head to stop her words, clearly wanting to be the one to take the lead. "I have one final dare for you, Chloe," he said, his voice low, gruff and just aggressive enough to pique her interest. "I want you. My room. My way. All night long."

She shivered, the promise of pleasure and ecstasy implicit in his proposition. Her answer came without any hesitation whatsoever. *"Yes."*

7

As soon as they stepped into Aiden's hotel room and the door shut behind them, Chloe found herself pressed against the nearest wall with his lips claiming hers in a deep, toe-curling kiss. He skimmed his hands along her curves, palms hard, seeking and propriety. Just the way she liked it.

Reaching the hem of her dress, he pulled the material upward, and she lifted her arms so he could pull it off in one smooth motion, leaving her clad in just her bra, panties and heels. His seductive mouth came back to hers again, his need and hunger matching hers as she eagerly shoved his jacket off his shoulders and helped him out of his shirt, until she was finally able to touch his naked chest.

His skin was hot and firm, the muscles in his abdomen flexing as she dragged her palms all the way down to the waistband of his slacks. Beyond anxious to feel the thick length of his erection in her hands, she fumbled with his belt, trying desperately to release the strip of leather from the buckle so she could unzip his pants.

A rough groan rumbled in his chest, and he grasped both of her wrists and pinned her hands at the sides of her head. He abruptly ended their kiss and rested his forehead against hers, their panting breaths mingling.

"We need to slow this down," he rasped in a hoarse voice.

She rolled her hips toward his, teasing and tempting him the best she could. "Why?"

Bracing his strong thighs against hers to keep her in place, which also served to nudge the impressive ridge of his erection against her belly, he nuzzled the side of her neck with his warm, soft lips. "Because I want to savor everything about this night."

A full-bodied shiver shimmied through her. She turned her head to the side, giving his mouth better access to her throat, and anything else he wanted. She understood his need to enjoy every moment, because there would be no repeat performances once they returned to Boston and their respective campaigns. But right now, she was anxious and impatient and slow seemed…well, too damned slow.

"We can do slow later," she said, groaning as he nipped her earlobe. "You put me right to the edge of an orgasm at dinner and I'm dying for it."

He lifted his head and stared down at her, his expression both pleased and cocky. There were no lights on in his room, but the drapes were wide open and an ample amount of moonlight spilled in, illuminating his gorgeous features and the wicked glint in his eyes.

"All in good time, Reiss," he murmured, and released her hands so they fell back to her sides. "My way, remember? And we've got the rest of the night to do it a dozen other ways. But right now, I want to take my time, because there are so many things I want to do to you...improper, indecent, down-and-dirty things I've thought about since the day we met."

His arousing promise made her wetter than she already was. Oh, yeah, she wanted those things, too. With effort, she kept her palms flattened against the wall behind her, letting him do this *his way* because she knew the end result would be pure, mind-blowing pleasure for both of them.

"What kind of improper, indecent, down-and-dirty things?" she asked, eager to experience each and every one.

"Things like this..." He slipped his fingers beneath the straps of her bra and pulled them down her arms. His mouth touched her skin, and he unexpectedly bit the curve of her neck and shoulder with his teeth.

She gasped at the light twinge of pain, enjoying his uncivilized behavior when he was a man who always came across as so refined and sophisticated in the boardroom.

"And this," he continued seductively as he unhooked her bra, letting it fall to the floor, then filled both of his hands with her breasts. His piercing gaze held hers as he cupped and squeezed the mounds of flesh, while his thumbs brushed over her taut nipples, then lightly pinched them.

She groaned, so turned on she could barely stand.

His eyes smoldered, and his wholly satisfied smile made those secret muscles deep inside her clench in anticipation as he lowered his head and claimed her breast. His tongue swirled around her areola, his teeth rasping and teasing the rigid tip before he drew her nipple into the damp heat of his mouth and sucked hard.

There was no holding back the cry of delight that escaped her lips, or the path of fire he created as his hand trailed down her body and slipped past the elastic waistband of her panties.

"And especially *this,*" he murmured against her breast, and with a skillful stroke of his fingers along her swollen, throbbing clitoris, he had her thighs quivering and her heart racing.

That quickly, her body screamed for release, but she knew he wasn't done tormenting her just yet. She closed her eyes, let her head fall back against the wall, and lost her breath when he pushed one, then two fingers, tight and hot inside her body.

His knee wedged between her thighs, coaxing them apart. "Spread your legs wider for me, sweetheart," he commanded and without hesitation she did exactly what he asked, widening her stance for him so that he was better able to thrust deeper.

In...then out. Slowly. Leisurely. His thumb circling, stroking. Again and again, while his mouth and tongue continued its sensual assault on her breasts. Her juices flowed, hot and inviting, adding a slick friction to his intimate invasion. Each enticing caress drove her out of her mind with the excruciating need to climax. Every erotic slide of his fingers made her helpless to do anything but ache for the orgasm he held just out of her reach.

His mouth came back up to her neck, his breath hot against her ear. "You're so warm, so soft and wet."

Moaning softly, she arched against his hand the best she could, craving more. "Stop teasing me."

She felt his lips curve into a smile against her cheek. "Tell me what you want, Chloe, and I'll give it to you."

The dominating edge to his voice, combined with the way he'd already mastered her body, was enough to make her beg without shame. "Please let me come," she whispered, and gasped as he finally gave her exactly what she desired.

He kissed her, his tongue sweeping into her mouth as his fingers plunged deeper, harder, faster, and the pad of his thumb rubbed that sweet, sensitive spot that sent liquid fire rushing through her veins. She clutched at his broad shoulders, her fingers digging into the taut muscles of his back in an attempt to hold on as the tension spiraled tighter and tighter inside her. Suddenly, it was all too much, and she moaned against his lips as an overwhelming climax rippled through her in strong, shuddering waves of rapture.

In the aftermath, her legs buckled, and Aiden wrapped an arm around her waist to give her the support she seemed to need. He lifted his head, that smug, cocky smile on his face, despite the fact that he was still as hard as stone against her belly. "You okay?"

She drew a steadying breath, nodded and gave him the praise he deserved. "I have to admit, *your way* isn't half bad."

He lifted an arrogant brow. "And just think, we're not even close to being done. We've only covered improper and indecent, and I'm *so* looking forward to getting down-and-dirty."

Oh, Lord, so was she.

He guided her to the bed. "Make yourself comfortable. I'll be right back."

As he disappeared into the bathroom, she slipped off her heels, shimmied out of her panties and settled against the pillows. Seconds later he returned with a few foil packets, and he tossed all but one of them onto the pillow beside her. Judging by how many condoms he'd retrieved, he obviously planned on having a very busy night with her. Not that she was complaining.

He stood at the foot of the bed, and she watched as he stripped off the rest of his clothes. He toed off his shoes and removed his socks, then unbuckled his thin leather belt. With a sexy smile on his lips, he unbuttoned and unzipped his slacks, then pushed his pants and briefs down his legs.

Completely naked, she looked her fill of him and sighed with female appreciation. If she thought he was gorgeous in a business suit at work, he was a perfect Adonis wearing nothing at all—lean, muscled and impressively endowed where it counted most. His strong, capable hands sheathed his erection, the sight of him touching his cock adding to the eroticism of the act.

He came up on the mattress, circled his fingers around her ankles and separated her feet until she was sufficiently spread for him. Settling between her legs, he dipped his head and brushed his lips along her inner thigh, making it very clear what he had in mind next.

"Let's see if you taste as good as a peach," he murmured, and used his thumbs to separate her folds so he could sweep his tongue along her sex, licking her with such thorough reverence she felt worshipped.

His fingers joined in, penetrating her aching core. He sucked on her clit as if she were as ripe and juicy as the fruit he'd indicated, then traced his tongue all along her swollen, sensitive flesh before starting the devastatingly erotic process all over again. Multiple times. Her entire body trembled and when he finally let her come, the release was more than just physical—it was beyond anything she'd ever experienced before.

Moaning softly, she reached down and threaded her fingers through his soft, silky hair, unable to recall when a man had ever taken such time and care with her, instead of racing to the main event. Even now, he was nuzzling her thigh and giving her time to catch her breath. It was an intimate act, and more than just about getting her off so he could take his own pleasure. He'd enjoyed going down on her, reveled in her response even, and for that he received extra points.

He straightened and knelt between her legs, his gaze taking a slow, leisurely journey from her thighs all the way up to her face. "That was fun," he said huskily. "And now that we've gotten 'down' out of the way, it's time to get dirty."

In a move that caught her by surprise, he rolled her over so that she was on her stomach, then grasped her hips and pulled her toward him, until she was positioned on her hand and knees, his intentions very clear.

Excitement coursed through her. Obviously, traditional, missionary sex was too tame for a sexual God like him. This position put him in control and fed into the fantasy she'd revealed to him on the plane… where she'd confessed her preference of being taken by a man, aggressively and passionately.

He caressed his palms over her bare butt and squeezed the mounds in his hands. "You have the sweetest, sexiest ass. When you wear a tight skirt at the office, I can't help but stare and fantasize about what it would be like to do this." His fingers traced the crease separating her cheeks, then stroked her inner lips, gliding through her slick heat, driving her crazy until she was on fire for him again.

"And what it would be like to do this," he said, and thrust his cock into her, his thick length stretching her in the best possible way.

They groaned in unison, and she went down on her forearms so that her back was completely arched, allowing him to slide even deeper inside her. With his hands at her waist again, he plunged into her, hard and fast, her body clutching around him hungrily, eagerly.

Another round of tension coiled low and tight in her groin, shocking her. She'd thought he'd wrung everything out of her with those two explosive orgasms, but apparently not, because she started to shake and quiver anew. She fisted the bed covers in her hands, desperate for something to anchor her in a sea of overwhelming sensation.

Behind her, Chloe felt Aiden's restraint start to unravel as he began pumping against her in earnest. His hips surged forward, driving every last inch into her, and she cried out as blissful waves of ecstasy contracted through her, and around Aiden's shaft. Seconds later, a harsh groan vibrated in his chest as he gave himself over to his own powerful orgasm.

He collapsed on top of her, bracing his forearms on either side of her head to keep his weight from crushing her. Still buried deep inside her, he pressed his face against her neck, the scent of his body and down-and-dirty sex surrounding them as their heart rates gradually slowed.

"God, you're even more incredible than I imagined," he rasped against her ear.

An exhausted, incredulous laugh escaped her. He'd just given her three amazing orgasms with utmost enthusiasm, had made her body sing in ways it never had before, and he was complimenting *her?* Unbelievable. *He* was the one who was incredible. And addictive, because now that she knew how good they were together, how was she ever going to give this, and him, up?

She immediately shook that unbidden thought from her mind, just as Aiden rolled off of her and got to his feet. He disappeared for a quick moment into the bathroom to take care of the condom and then he was back, pulling her into his arms, spooning her backside against his chest and thighs.

As nice as cuddling with him was, Chloe suddenly felt an overwhelming sense of apprehension brought on by his physical display of affection. Tonight was supposed to be about *sex,* no post-coital snuggling and getting close involved. And being held in his arms felt much too intimate. It made her feel exposed and vulnerable.

She swallowed hard. Giving her an orgasm while pinning her against the wall was just the way she liked things...aggressive and hot. But *this* was so much more than she'd bargained for with Aiden, and something warned her that falling for him, beyond this coworkers-with-benefits-for-a-few-days arrangement of theirs, wouldn't be difficult to do. And that kind of attachment was something she could never allow—personally or professionally.

Needing space, she tried to wriggle away, but he tightened his arm around her waist, oblivious to her internal distress.

"Stay put, Reiss," he said gruffly. "I'm not finished with you yet. I just need about a half an hour to recharge."

I need to go. She swallowed back the panic rising within her, and tried to keep things light and superficial until she figured out a way to leave without making a scene. "What are you, the Energizer Bunny?"

He chuckled and replied drowsily. "Apparently, with you I am."

She said nothing more, and within a few minutes she felt his body go lax and the rise and fall of his chest deepen. And even though the arm he'd secured around her loosened, her lungs seemed to burn with every breath she struggled to take.

Good Lord, she was going to hyperventilate! What the hell was wrong with her? The crazy temptation to stay the night warred with a deeper common sense. While a part of her liked the warmth and security his embrace provided—it had been much too long since a man had just curled up with her after sex—it was nothing more than a false sense of security. Besides, all this intimate, emotional crap slipping beneath the surface of her skin wasn't what their agreed upon affair was all about, and she'd do well to remember that.

She waited another few minutes, until he relaxed once again and a soft snore rumbled from his chest before she gently lifted his arm and slowly moved off the bed. Leaving the lights off, she found her clothes and slipped her dress back on, sans underwear, and picked up her shoes from the floor. Then she made her way to the door.

If he heard her slip out of the room, this time he didn't try to stop her, and she was relieved and grateful.

THE NEXT MORNING, Aiden strolled into the dining room for the complimentary brunch the resort provided for its guests, surprised to find Chloe already there. She was sitting alone at a table at the far end of the room near a window overlooking one of the tropical gardens outside, eating her breakfast while writing something in a notebook—probably notes for their campaign. That's exactly how he'd spent the past few hours, working on his own presentation and how to best use Hattie-the-matchmaker as his focal point for the campaign.

His stomach grumbled ravenously, demanding to be fed, and he headed straight for the omelet bar and put in his order, then piled his plate high with bacon, fruit and other side dishes. He filled a large glass with orange juice and added a cup of coffee to his tray, then carried his hearty meal toward Chloe's table.

He honestly wasn't sure what to expect from her this morning, not after the way she'd snuck out on him last night while he'd been dozing. The soft click of the door shutting had woken him up, and he'd instinctively known that she was gone. He'd gotten as far as tossing off the sheets and grabbing his pants to put them on so he could go after her, before realizing he'd be chasing after a woman who clearly didn't want to be pursued.

The thought was a much needed reality check that this thing between them was nothing more than a casual island fling. He had no claim to her other than just sex. But he'd be lying if he said that being with Chloe was nothing more than an itch he'd been dying to scratch for the past two years.

Oh, they'd definitely indulged in a whole lot of pleasure, had finally surrendered wholeheartedly to the lust that had burned bright and hot between them for much too long. But afterward, as he'd pulled her into his arms, he'd been filled with a contentment that wasn't all related to his physical satisfaction. It had more to do with how good and right she felt in his arms—more than any woman he'd been with since his divorce.

That realization was like a sucker punch to his stomach and definitely got his attention—because his mind had no business contemplating those thoughts with her. Ever. No matter what the island matchmaker, or the stamen of a flower, revealed.

So, while Aiden was disappointed with Chloe's stealthlike exit last night, he understood why she'd felt the need to leave. She was trying to keep some semblance of normalcy between them, to keep their affair separate from the fact that they still worked together, at an agency that frowned heavily on inter-office romances. It didn't matter that he intended to leave the company within the next few months, especially if he was the recipient of the five-figure bonus that would be awarded to the St. Raphael campaign winner. He and Chloe were opposites in all the important ways that mattered, which meant they had no future together beyond this week.

As he neared her table, she glanced up while taking a drink of her coffee, her eyes widening ever so slightly over the rim of her cup as she watched him approach. Wearing her hair in one of her sleek ponytails, she looked beautiful and fresh-faced, and he'd like to believe that the three orgasms he'd given her last night had something to do with the pink glow on her cheeks.

Yeah, he was totally going to take credit for that.

She was wearing a pair of white shorts, a pink lace tank top and sparkly flip-flops, trying to blend in with every other woman in the dining room. But to him, she stood out like an exotic fruit he wanted to taste—again and again.

Not wanting to risk a rejection until he got a feel

for her mood, he didn't bother asking if she wanted company, just set his tray down on the table and took a seat across from her. She said nothing, but the wary look in her gaze told him that she fully expected an interrogation about giving him the slip after last night's sexcapades. Lucky for her, he wasn't going to complain about it. Hell, he wasn't even going to mention the issue because it was a discussion they didn't need to have.

His plan was to keep things between them light, casual and fun. No morning-after angst necessary.

Scooping up a forkful of his omelet, he nodded toward her notebook. "Already hard at work?"

She shrugged and relaxed somewhat, her obvious relief softening her features. "I had some ideas about a catchy slogan running through my head that I wanted to get on paper before I forgot the words. I always swear I'm going to remember a brilliant idea because it's so ingenious, but if I don't write it down, it slips right through my mind."

He caught the small inkling of a smile teasing the corner of her mouth, a positive sign that things were getting back to normal between the two of them. "I hate when that happens."

She eyed the massive amount of food on his plate. "Somebody is hungry this morning."

He finished eating a piece of bacon and chased it down with a mouthful of coffee, seeing in her eyes that she was teasing him. She clearly had a knack for compartmentalizing sex and work—maybe better than he could because when he looked at her mouth, all he could think about was how he enjoyed kissing her. And not just on the lips, because she tasted sweet *everywhere.* He knew that for a fact now.

He grinned wolfishly and waggled his brows at her. "What can I say? I worked up an appetite last night."

She laughed and dropped her gaze to the slice of cantaloupe she'd picked up with her fingers, examining it more than necessary before taking a bite. She chewed, then spoke. "Speaking of last night, I think we need to establish some rules."

"Okay," he said, and waited for her to steer this conversation in whatever direction she felt necessary.

She licked the remnants of fruit juice off her fingers, making his gut clench with that familiar burn of desire for her. "I just want to be sure that we're on the same page with this temporary affair."

It was a legitimate enough request, and he simplified things for the both of them. "How about what happens at this resort, stays at this resort?" It was a clichéd line, but so appropriate to their situation. "Once we're on the plane back to Boston, we leave it all behind and chalk it up to one helluva good time together. Then we go back to the way things were. Simple, easy and uncomplicated."

Something that looked suspiciously like disappointment flashed in her eyes, then was quickly gone. "Agreed," she said with a succinct nod of her head.

Rules were good, he told himself, and the one he'd just established put things between them back into proper perspective and gave them free rein to indulge in their desires and fantasies. "So, that still gives us four more days to enjoy each other, including today," he said, even as a tiny part of him wondered if he'd be able to get enough of her in that short amount of time.

She flashed him a seductive smile full of promise. "I'm looking forward to it." Finished with the rest of her fruit, she wiped her hands on her napkin. "I have a full schedule of things I need to do today to prepare for my campaign, including meeting with the photographer and the couple he hired for us to use in our shots, but tonight we have a choice between attending a toga party or a masquerade ball. What's your pleasure?" she asked, her tone flirtatious.

"You," he said without hesitation, infusing the one word with erotic intent. "Any way I can have you."

She bit her bottom lip, her gaze flaring with reciprocal lust. "Well, since you had your way with me last night, I think it's only fair that I get my turn this evening."

Oh, hell yeah. Her invitation sent a rush of heat and anticipation through his veins, the kind that would undoubtedly have him spending most the day in a mild state of sexual frustration. "I can't wait."

"Me, either," she practically purred as she rested her chin in her hand. "So, what'll it be. Toga or masquerade?"

Since a toga party reminded him too much of his college fraternity days, he opted for something more low-key. "I vote for the masquerade party."

"Mmm. That would be my choice, as well," she said, her voice laced with approval. "It's perfect for a little mystery and seduction."

Her eyes—dark, sultry and teasing—told him that she was already thinking about all the ways to use that to her advantage.

"In the meantime, I have work to do." She stood up, grabbed her notebook and smiled at him. "I'll see you later, Landry."

He watched the sweet sway of her ass as she walked away, his incorrigible mind filling with the arousing memories of how he'd taken her last night. He groaned to himself and was grateful when she finally disappeared from his view.

He finished his breakfast and decided to use his time wisely and get some work done, too. He had a meeting with Ricardo, the photographer, after Chloe's appointment, and he wanted to find the most opportune places to stage some pictures that would best elevate his visual presentation and showcase his marketing ideas for the St. Raphael Resort.

But first, he wanted to talk to Hattie again, to see if he could figure out the best way to merge her traditional matchmaking methods with the resort's current contemporary approach. Five minutes later, he entered the humid greenhouse and found Hattie talking to another young couple, and he hung back so as not to interrupt their conversation.

Hattie was dressed in yet another cheerful caftan dress, but today she'd worn her long braids down. They were entwined with tiny red flowers, and the length of them nearly reached her waist. As soon as she saw him, her eyes lit up with pleasure, though she didn't approach him until after the other man and woman left the greenhouse.

"You came back, but where is the pretty woman you were with yesterday?" she asked, tipping her head curiously. "Did I scare her off with my bold prediction that the two of you belong together?"

He chuckled. Chloe didn't scare easily, and despite the other woman's claims, he knew the only way he and Chloe would ever be *together* was between the sheets. And as he'd discovered last night, that wasn't a bad place to be with a woman as passionate as Chloe.

"Chloe had other things she needed to do," he explained easily. "I'm here because I'd like to talk to you about your matchmaking abilities. I think the resort's advertising could really benefit by utilizing you and that hybrid flower as an added draw, to romanticize the island and give guests an extraordinary experience they can't get elsewhere. It's a great marketing angle."

Hattie's brows furrowed into a frown. "Tell me something. Do *you* believe I have the ability to know when two people are meant for one another?"

Not wanting to offend the older woman, Aiden thought carefully about his answer before he spoke. "I think your intentions are honest and real, and I think that most people want to find that one special person, which makes it easy for them to believe in your intuition. When it comes to marketing and advertising, that's all that matters."

"What made you so skeptical when it comes to love?" she asked, her tone softening as she tended to the potted plant between them.

He shrugged, not wanting to get into a discussion about his failed marriage and bitter divorce with a woman he barely knew. "I'm just practical when it comes to certain things." Like his feelings for Chloe, which did not include love or a future together. "But that doesn't mean others wouldn't benefit from your knowledge and instincts."

She considered that for a moment as she watered the plant, then met his gaze, a secretive type smile on her lips. "I'll agree to be a part of this marketing angle you want to use for your campaign, and maybe, by the time you leave the island, you'll see for yourself that my prediction about you and Chloe is true, that the two of you are meant for one another."

"Fair enough," he said, though he already knew that Hattie was going to be sorely disappointed, because despite him and Chloe being sexually compatible, that's all there would ever be between them.

8

A WHILE LATER, when Aiden met up with Ricardo at their designated time, Chloe was nowhere to be seen. Aiden discussed the shots he wanted with the photographer, and they started their session with candid pictures of the different activities the resort had to offer. He arranged shots of the professional couple having drinks at the underwater bar at the pool, then on to a more romantic setting of them in one of the upgraded bungalows away from the main hotel. Lastly, they did a fun, playful session of the couple at the beach and frolicking in the ocean.

Aiden figured in the next few days he'd have Ricardo take some pictures of Hattie for him to add to his presentation, and he planned to tape a short video interview with her, too. The more the idea of focusing on the sentimental notion of a traditional matchmaker took shape in his mind, the more enthusiastic he became about the entire concept. Aiden didn't yet know what ideas Chloe was considering for her presentation, but he was confident that he'd be giving the resort a unique and distinctive point of view that would ultimately award him the account. As far as he was concerned, he didn't have to personally believe in Hattie's intuitive nature in order to pitch a convincing and effective campaign.

A few hours passed to midafternoon, and just when Ricardo called the final session a wrap and his crew began packing up all their equipment, Aiden caught sight of Chloe making her way down the pathway to the beach, clearly intending to enjoy the rest of her day now that her work was done. She was wearing a white cover-up and flip-flops, and was carrying a canvas tote bag. She headed toward the private cabanas set up on the sand, not even noticing him standing beneath a large palm tree with Ricardo, in the opposite direction.

As he waited for Ricardo to finish talking to the models, Aiden's gaze strayed back to Chloe, who'd found a vacant cabana with two lounge chairs. She was peeling off her white frock. He nearly swallowed his tongue when she revealed the itty-bitty turquoise bikini that showcased her amazing figure. The top drew his attention to her full, pert breasts, and the tiny bottoms accentuated her slim hips and long, slender legs. She bent over to retrieve her suntan lotion from her bag, then began rubbing the silky oil along her shoulders, arms and chest, over her flat stomach, her thighs, her calves—making him wish he was with her to do the deed himself.

Once she was finished, she angled her chaise so it was in the sun, then reclined on the chair, her entire body glistening in the sunlight like a tempting offering to all mankind.

He bit back a groan of appreciation, and noticed a few other guys in the area casting surreptitious, lust-filled glances her way, too. A possessive emotion spiked through him, along with an unwanted urge to head over to Chloe to establish ownership of a woman that wasn't his—other than sexually, and for only four more days.

You are such an idiot, Landry. Annoyed with himself and his barbaric, antiquated thoughts of claiming Chloe, he scrubbed a hand along his jaw and released a tension-filled breath, which did nothing to ease his internal frustration.

"You've got your hands full with that one."

Ricardo's comment snapped Aiden out of his silent thoughts and he redirected his attention back to the photographer. "Excuse me?" he asked, unsure what the guy meant.

Ricardo grinned in an all-knowing male way. "She has a lot of drive and ambition, in a way that's going to keep a guy on his toes."

Didn't he know it. Professionally, the competition between them had always pushed him to excel, and now personally, he was beginning to feel challenged, as well. And not in a good way. "I've worked with her for two years and she definitely makes me bring my A-game to the table."

Ricardo chuckled as he removed the long lens from his camera and packed it gently in a padded bag. "I bet she does. She said the two of you are competing for this account."

"Yep." He nodded, though it was hard to forget that another ad agency also had a hat in the ring. But for Aiden, his only true competition was Chloe. "The end results should be…interesting."

"Well, good luck with the campaign. And Chloe," Ricardo said meaningfully, a man-to-man look in his eyes. "Having an exciting woman in your life to keep you from becoming complacent isn't a bad thing."

Obviously the other man had seen the way he'd looked at Chloe just a few minutes ago, but Ricardo didn't know his history when it came to women. One in particular—the one he'd chosen to marry. A woman who'd been vibrant, exciting and had provided enough challenges to always keep him guessing. A woman who'd completely destroyed a part of him with her selfish decision to put her career aspirations before anything else in her life, including their marriage vows to honor and respect one another.

Paige had completely shattered his trust, and putting that kind of faith in a woman again was a huge issue he'd carried with him since the divorce. While Paige had walked away without looking back and had gone on to climb the corporate ladder with a high-ranking firm in New York, she'd left Aiden questioning his judgment.

"Looks like a vulture is circling," Ricardo said

in amusement, his gaze trained in the direction of Chloe once again.

Aiden turned his head so quickly he came close to giving himself whiplash. Sure enough, a young guy—shirtless, buff and cocky-looking—was walking up to where Chloe was laid out like a gorgeous, glistening goddess. It was then that he noticed that she wasn't wearing her red wristband, making her free game for the single men at the resort.

Nope. Not gonna happen. She was his…at least for a few more days and nights. That was his excuse, and he was sticking to it.

"Thanks for today, Ricardo," he said, and shook the other man's hand, eager to be on his way. "I'm looking forward to seeing the proofs."

"We got some great shots," the other man said, clearly enjoying Aiden's sudden interest in getting to Chloe. "I'll get them edited and to you on a flash drive by tomorrow afternoon so you can use them for your campaign."

"That's perfect."

Finished with his own work for the afternoon, Aiden followed the pathway to Chloe's lounge chair, his irritation growing as he watched her smile at the other man as he talked to her. She said something to make him laugh, and Aiden thought he'd pop a blood vessel. *Shit.*

Trying not to grind his molars, he stepped up to Chloe's cabana, determined to send her admirer on his way as quickly as possible. The guy frowned at him, as if *Aiden* were the interloper, and not him.

Aiden assumed an assertive stance next to Chloe's chair. "She's already taken." The tone of his voice was equally brusque.

The other guy dropped his gaze to Chloe, waiting for her to confirm or deny Aiden's statement. After a moment she sighed and offered her Romeo an apologetic smile. "Yes, I'm with him."

Immediately, the man held up his hands and backed away, looking contrite. "I didn't know. She wasn't wearing a red band."

She glanced up at Aiden from her reclining chair, her expression reflecting a hint of humor. "I didn't want a tan line."

As soon as the other man was gone, a smile twitched at the corner of her lovely, sensual mouth. "What was *that* all about?" she asked.

Hands on his hips, he shrugged, trying to keep his gaze on her face, instead of leering at her gorgeous breasts, barely concealed by a scrap of bright blue fabric. "Just trying to save you from the buzzards."

She rolled her eyes. "I don't need saving. I'm not some damsel in distress who needs a white knight to rescue her."

Of course she didn't. "When I'm with someone, I don't share."

She laughed at him, the sound light and teasing. "That's a bit of a caveman mentality, don't you think?"

"Caveman?" He smirked, recalling just how she'd liked being manhandled last night. "I'll show you *caveman.*"

He pulled off his shirt, then scooped her off the lounge chair and up into his arms. She squealed in surprise, and he grinned as he bounced her and shifted her quickly so that she was slung over his shoulder—caveman style.

A shocked gasp escaped her. "Are you kidding me?"

She squirmed against his shoulder, her slippery, oil-slicked body making it more difficult for him to keep her in place. He locked his arm tight across the back of her knees so she couldn't slide off him, and started down the beach to the ocean. "Does it look like I'm kidding you?"

She tried to kick her feet, all to no avail. Then she smacked his ass. Hard. "Put me down, Landry!"

"Oh, I will," he drawled as he wrapped a hand around her smooth, supple thigh and gave it an affectionate squeeze. He'd release her just as soon as she had a soft surface in which to land.

"Oooh, you are so going to pay for this!"

Considering she was laughing, her threat lacked any true animosity. "I'm sure I will, and I'm looking forward to it," he said, just as he reached the water—and continued wading in until the gentle waves lapped around the hem of his shorts.

"I'm warning you, Landry," she said, exasperation and defiance mingling in her stern tone. "Do not do this!"

"Sorry, babe," he said as he maneuvered her body so she was once again in his arms and he was grinning down at her. "But I really can't resist."

Effortlessly, he tossed her into the clear blue ocean—her arms flailing, eyes wide, and a garbled "arrghhh!" rending the air before she dropped into the water with a satisfying splash, then sank below the surface.

She came up sputtering, wet strands of hair in her face, and he couldn't restrain his deep, throaty chuckle as he started back out of the water. Damn, but that felt good.

"Oh, no you don't," she said from behind him. "You're not getting away until you get dunked, too."

The next thing he knew she'd jumped onto his back and wrapped her arms and legs around him like a monkey. And while he could have kept on walking, he decided to have some fun instead. He let her take him down to the water, just so she felt as though she'd gotten even. When he came up for air, she was trying to swim away, and he went after her for a playful game of chase—giving her a bit of leeway before he caught her in his arms once again.

This time, she came willingly, her carefree laughter making him chuckle, too. He was chest deep in the water, and she entwined her arms around his neck and secured her legs around his waist, clinging to him for support as she fisted her fingers in his damp hair and settled her mouth over his and kissed him…slowly, deeply, thoroughly.

Beneath the water, he cupped her bottom in his hands and pulled her closer, so that his growing erection rubbed between her legs. She groaned blissfully against his lips before ending the heated, lust-fueled kiss and stared into his eyes.

"God, you are so hot and sexy," she breathed. "I can't wait to do you tonight."

He raised a brow. "Do me?"

"Oh, yeah," she said with a nod, her bright green/brown eyes promising all sorts of wicked pleasure. "I'm going to *do you* in ways that are going to make you forget every other woman."

It was quite a claim, but he believed her…because right now, just being with Chloe like this, so playful, flirtatious and incredibly sexy, no other woman existed for him. He wanted her, any way he could have her. For as long as their time together allowed.

"How about a preview?" he teased, wondering if she'd be that bold and brazen, even with them submersed in the ocean.

She shook her head, the long, wet strands of her hair tickling across his bare chest. "I don't want to get kicked off the resort for public indecency."

She was so fun and uninhibited, and he loved seeing this lighthearted side of her, outside of work and all the rules and restrictions that had forced them to suppress their attraction for way too long. "Then give me a hint of what I can expect."

"It will include a lot of licking," she said, as she dipped her head and dragged her tongue along the side of his neck. "And probably some biting..." Her teeth gently nibbled along his jaw to his mouth. "And especially *sucking.*"

He groaned like a dying man as she rolled his bottom lip between her teeth and applied enough of a soft, wet suction to inspire all kinds of provocative images in his head. His cock, already standing at attention, grew hard as stone, and there was no doubt in his mind that she felt every inch.

She pulled back and blinked at him guilelessly, as if she hadn't just elevated his internal temperature by ten degrees. "Is that enough of a hint for you?"

"Oh, hell yeah," he said huskily. "You had me at licking. Though biting and sucking are good, too."

She laughed. "You, Mr. Landry, are so *easy.*"

He couldn't argue with that, because he was coming to realize that when it came to her, he was easily persuaded, influenced and seduced.

DRINK IN HAND, Aiden casually strolled through the crush of people at the masquerade ball, searching for Chloe in the sea of singles and couples attending the formal affair. Like most of the other men at the party, he'd worn a black suit, while the women were dressed in an array of formal cocktail dresses and elegant gowns ranging in color from basic black to bright jewel tones.

Upon entering the ballroom, everyone had been

required to choose a mask to wear for the evening, and there had been a wide selection to pick from—ones with glitter and jewels, some that looked like butterflies, and others decorated with elaborate feathers, ribbons or lace. Not one for frills, he'd opted for the simple black gentleman's mask, which concealed the upper half of his face.

Music played and a huge buffet of food and desserts were on display for guests, but the only thing Aiden was interested in was finding Chloe. Considering how difficult it was to identify the women wearing masks, he questioned the wisdom of agreeing to meet her here, instead of them coming together.

"Hey, sugar, care to dance?"

Aiden turned toward the petite brunette who'd come up to his side, her blue eyes inquiring beneath the pearl-and-sequin mask hiding her face. She appeared pretty enough, but seemed to be trying overly hard to attract a man in the skintight, strapless, bust-enhancing purple dress she was wearing that screamed *look at my breasts*.

Not even a flicker of interest passed through him, because the only woman on his mind was Chloe. Yeah, he had it bad for her. "Sorry, but I'm with someone," he told the other woman, indicating the red band on his wrist.

She sighed, her lips pursed in disappointment. "I should have known someone as hot as you would already be taken. It seems all the good ones have already been snatched up."

Aiden watched in amusement as the woman continued on her quest to find an unattached guy. Most people had paired off, but there were a few singles still mingling. He supposed not everyone would leave the resort having found someone they wanted to pursue once their time on the island was over.

He absently swirled his scotch in his glass, his gaze stopping on a woman making her way through the crowd and heading toward him. There was no doubt in his mind that it was Chloe, and his body instantly tightened in awareness. He knew that slow, sexy walk of hers that made her hips sway oh-so-sensually, and recognized the compact curves beneath the black dress she wore. A mask with colorful feathers covered most of her features, and while he couldn't see her face, the seductive smile on her lips was pure, provocative Chloe.

Clearly recognizing him, as well, she stopped in front of him and curled her fingers in the lapels of his jacket. Without preamble she tilted her head to the side and settled her mouth against his, kissing him like a woman with a purpose—to drive him out of his mind with wanting her.

He was already there.

Sliding her tongue along his one last time, she ended the mind-bending kiss, and just as mysteriously as she'd materialized, she turned back around and walked away. Seconds later, she vanished into the crush of party revelers—leaving him dazed and intrigued by her flirtatious game of hide-and-seek.

Grinning, he headed in the direction she'd just disappeared, knowing he'd spend the entire night trying to find her if that's what it took. Fortunately, his search only lasted a few minutes, until one of the waiters serving champagne handed him a small sealed envelope with his name on it.

"I was instructed to give this to you."

Recognizing the handwriting as Chloe's, Aiden accepted the note. "Thank you." Breaking the seal, he pulled out a card and read the message she'd written for him.

I want to be your fantasy come true. My room. My way.

God, she already *was* his deepest, most erotic fantasy come to life, and there was no way he could resist her invitation. Tucking the card into his jacket pocket, he removed his mask and left the masquerade ball, his final destination Chloe's hotel room. A few minutes later, he was knocking on her door, his pulse pounding in anticipation of what the night would bring.

Chloe opened the door, now dressed in a deep purple, thigh-length silky robe, her mask gone, though he was pleased to see she was still wearing her black stiletto heels. With a sultry smile, she took his hand and pulled him inside. Somehow, she'd gotten a hold of some candles, which were placed around the room, the flickering flames creating a warm, romantic glow of light. The intoxicating scent of vanilla filled the air, and soft mood-music played from her iPod on the dresser, adding to the seductive atmosphere.

"First, let's get *you* out of some of your clothes," she said, her eyes alight with promise as she pulled his suit jacket off and draped it over the back of one of the desk chairs.

While he toed off his shoes, she tugged on his tie, loosening the strip of material enough to remove it over his head, then she began unbuttoning his shirt and slipped the crisp white cotton over his shoulders and down his arms. He removed his socks, and when he started to unbuckle his thin black belt, she grabbed his wrists and stopped him.

"Leave your pants on," she said, leaning into him to gently nip at his bottom lip. "For now."

"Yes, ma'am," he murmured, letting her run tonight's show without any objection from him.

"Sit on that chair by the bed," she told him, indicating the other desk chair she'd positioned there.

Her request ramped up his curiosity another level as he walked around to the side of the bed. Withdrawing three foil packets from his slacks' pocket, he set them on the nightstand and flashed her one of his charming smiles. "I'm hoping we'll be needing these at some point tonight."

A flirtatious smile touched the corner of her mouth. "Maybe. If you're lucky."

Oh, he was feeling extremely lucky tonight. He

sat down, stretching his legs out in front of him, and clasped his hands over his stomach. He watched as she strolled back to the dresser, touched her iPod, and Kings of Leon's song, "Sex On Fire," started to play.

She slowly made her way back to him, her hips moving rhythmically, while every step she took allowed him a glimpse of creamy bare thigh peeking from the front opening of her robe. Oh-so-slowly, she tugged on the silky belt, letting the material part gradually as she performed a riveting striptease just for him. In time, she shrugged her shoulders and the robe fluttered to the floor at her feet, leaving her standing in front of him in a black lace bra, matching panties and those do-me heels.

It was all he could do to keep from grabbing her and pulling her onto his lap for a more private, intimate kind of dance.

Her fingers slid the straps of her bra down to her elbows, exposing the top swells of her breasts as she reached behind her and unhooked the closure. She straightened her arms, and the lacy fabric joined her robe on the floor, her firm, full breasts on glorious display.

He shifted in his seat as heat and arousal pumped through him, hardening his cock in a flash. The growing bulge in his pants didn't escape her notice, and when she licked her lips, he felt it all the way to his groin.

Christ, she was killing him…in the best way possible.

Closing her eyes, she lifted her arms above her head and started dancing provocatively for him—so confident, sexy and gorgeous. Candlelight flickered across her bare skin, caressing her breasts with a golden warmth as her entire body shimmied and her hips gyrated in time to the music, her every move sinuous and mesmerizing.

And then she began touching herself…

Her fingers threaded through her long, silky brown hair, then leisurely trailed along her throat. He bit back a groan as her hands cupped her breasts, lifting and playing with them, kneading the hard nipples until her lips parted with a soft gasp of pleasure that resonated through him.

Her lashes fluttered back open, and she stared at him, a wicked smile on her lips as her hands continued downward, skimming lightly, playfully, over her flat belly. Slender fingers dipped beneath the waistband of her panties, slid between her thighs and pressed inward. A deep breath shuddered out of her, leaving no doubt in his mind that those fingers were buried in the slick, wet heat of her own arousal. Right where *he* wanted to be.

Her eyes darkened with desire. "Remember that fantasy you told me about on the plane?"

As if he could forget revealing his biggest turn-on. "Watching a woman pleasure herself," he said.

She withdrew her hand and hooked her thumbs into the sides of her panties, pushing them down her legs and off, so that she was now completely naked.

Then she stepped out of her high heels and sat down on the bed directly in front of him, legs together.

God, she was gorgeous, and so damn sexy she stole his sanity and nearly obliterated his self-control. Her rich, dark hair cascaded over her shoulders to her breasts, her taut nipples peeking out through the silky strands. Her skin was flushed from her striptease, her eyes dilated with the kind of carnal lust that speared straight to his aching cock.

"I want to be that fantasy for you," she said huskily. "Tell me what you want me to do."

Her irresistible offer stunned him, and made him realize just how much thought she'd put into tonight's rendezvous. No other woman had ever been so uninhibited just for him, and he was glad that Chloe was going to be the one to fulfill this secret fantasy of his.

"Spread your legs and touch yourself," he said, his voice a low, growling demand. "Show me what makes you hot and wet."

"You do," she whispered as her thighs parted wide, giving him the unobstructed view he wanted.

He liked her answer, liked even more how she bit her plump bottom lip as her fingers parted her delicate pink flesh, then glided along her swollen clitoris in slow, lazy circles that caused her to shiver in delight.

"Deeper," he ordered huskily.

Her fingers, damp with her own desire, glided lower, until one penetrated her core, dipping and swirling rhythmically while her thumb continued to caress and stroke her cleft. Her breasts rose and fell, faster and deeper, matching the seductive dance of her fingers on her sex.

His body, already tense with need, was on fire for her. His dick was so hard it hurt, and it didn't help that it was confined inside his slacks. Desperately needing to ease the uncomfortable, building pressure, he unbuckled his belt, unzipped his pants and freed his erection from his boxer-briefs. His groan of relief caught Chloe's attention, and her hungry, lust-filled gaze dropped to his thick shaft.

"I want to watch you touch yourself, too," she murmured.

More than happy to oblige her request, he wrapped his fingers around his cock and began to stroke, root to tip. Slowly. Leisurely. A drop of moisture beaded on the head, and he dragged his thumb through the slick lubrication, using it to increase the friction, just enough to feel good without taking him over the edge.

Her gaze was riveted to his hand stroking his shaft, just as fascinated and aroused by the sight of him masturbating as he was with her display of eroticism.

"Oh, God, Aiden…"

Hearing the catch in her voice, and knowing she was on the verge of climaxing, he gave her that final push she seemed to need. "Let go and come for me, babe," he rasped.

Her fingers moved faster over her clitoris, her hips

jerking, her thighs trembling as her orgasm rocked through her. Tipping her head back, she closed her eyes and whimpered softly, losing herself in her own private world of ecstasy, while allowing him to be a voyeur to her pleasure.

He'd never witnessed anything so freaking hot and erotic, and his own climax surged forward, threatening to erupt. Not wanting to come until he was buried deep inside of her, he tightened his fingers around the base of his cock to keep his release at bay. More than anything he wanted to press her back on the bed and drive into her, but with effort, he held back.

It took her a few extra moments to come down from her high and regain her equilibrium, and when she did she moved off the bed and settled on her knees in front of where he was still sitting on the chair. She grabbed the sides of his pants and pulled downward, clearly wanting them off. He lifted his hips and let her undress him, until he was just as naked as she was.

Smiling like a woman who was about to blow his mind, she pressed her palms against his knees and pushed his legs apart. "This is where the licking, biting and sucking are about to happen," she said, reminding him of the promise she'd made this afternoon at the beach.

Leaning forward, she nibbled her way up the inside of his thigh, her breath damp and hot against his skin, and her teeth eliciting just enough of a sting to elevate his awareness of where she was heading. When she reached his shaft, her tongue came into play, licking a wet path all the way up to the sensitive tip. He groaned, tangling his hands in her hair, and with a devilish smile she wrapped her lips around the throbbing head and pulled him into the lush, silky heat of her mouth…all the way to the back of her throat.

Overwhelming lust pounded at him as her tongue swirled along the length of his cock, and then she sucked him, hard and deep, and he damn near exploded.

Considering how intensely aroused he was, this bit of foreplay was all he could handle without climaxing right then and there. Swearing beneath his breath, he fisted his hands in her hair and pulled her head back until she had no choice but to release him.

Eyes smoldering, she blinked up at him, surprised that he'd ended things so soon, and he quickly explained. "As tempting as your mouth is, I need to be inside you."

Need. Such a strong, emotional word. But that's what she made him feel…a desperate, undeniable demand to be a part of her that shook him to the core. And not just physically. Refusing to overanalyze things when this week was supposed to be nothing more than a fun, sexy affair, he shoved those thoughts and feelings out of his head. Right now, tonight, it was all about pleasure, and nothing more.

Unsure how she wanted to proceed, he let her

take the lead, knowing he'd do whatever she wanted because the end result would be the same no matter what—being buried deep inside her. She reached for one of the condoms on the nightstand and sheathed him. Then she stood back up, straddled his thighs, and with her hands gripping his shoulders and her gaze holding his, she slowly, gradually, sank onto his cock, the fit so tight and hot he didn't even try to stop the low, rough, possessive growl of *need* that escaped him.

He placed his hands at the small of her back as the music on her iPod changed to another feverish song, and she began moving to the heavy, driving beat in an erotic lap dance—her body grinding into his, hips gyrating, thighs clenching tight along his as she rode his shaft.

Moaning softly, she threaded her fingers into his hair, pulled his head back and settled her mouth over his, kissing him deeply, passionately, completely fusing the connection between them. Feeling her body clench around his cock, and knowing she was as close as he was to coming, he slid a hand between them and stroked her clitoris, triggering her release. He thrust upward and surrendered to the wild, intense pleasure pouring through him, while Chloe held on to him as if he were the only solid thing that still existed in a universe that had just tipped crazily on its axis.

He felt the same way and knew that no matter what they'd originally agreed upon when they'd arrived at the resort, things would never be the same between them again. And he wasn't quite sure what to do about that.

9

THE NEXT THREE days at the resort passed quickly for Chloe. The mornings and afternoons were filled with attending activities and working on her ad campaign and presentation, while her nights were spent with Aiden, fulfilling all sorts of fun fantasies and just enjoying one another. Yeah, that was definitely the best part of their time together, she thought as she cast a glance at Aiden where he sat across from her at the spacious boardroom table in one of the conference rooms that the hotel had given them to use during their stay at the resort.

Sex with Aiden was so off-the-charts hot, beyond anything she could have imagined or predicted, and just thinking of being with him made her go all warm and soft inside. Physically, they were incredibly in sync, but as the days passed, she was becoming increasingly aware of the fact that every time they were together, she became more emotionally involved, and that was something she never could have anticipated happening.

She continued to silently watch Aiden, very familiar with the slight crease of his brows that indicated he was deep in thought as he worked. His hair was tousled from being finger-combed, something he did when he was completely immersed in a project. He was wearing a casual T-shirt that clung to his broad shoulders, drawing her gaze to his toned biceps and strong forearms and how those muscles flexed as he typed a steady stream of information on his laptop.

She could sit for hours and marvel at how gorgeous and sexy he was, but that wouldn't be very productive for her, though she had accomplished quite a lot since they'd arrived earlier that afternoon. Chloe figured she deserved a break. Especially after the intense meeting they'd had with the vice president of the resort, Edward Luca, which had given them both the opportunity to ask pertinent questions about marketing strategies and objectives and get a better feel for what they envisioned for the future of the resort.

The knowledge they'd gleaned from Edward had been invaluable, but she and Aiden were still very aware of the fact that there was another ad agency on the island, and they'd had a meeting with the VP, as well. The pressure was on, because today was their last day to gather any last bits of information for their campaigns before flying back to Boston tomorrow.

She and Aiden had both used the large, flat surface of the conference table to spread out the visual presentation boards they'd created over the past few days that included the photographs that Ricardo had taken for them, along with their campaign theme and branding message that would complement their PowerPoint presentations. Chloe had yet to nail her slogan for the St. Raphael Resort; she wanted something simple yet nuanced, and while she had a few ideas in mind, nothing had yet to grab her in terms of giving the client that clear message that would resonate with their target audience.

The one thing she was extremely excited about was the flash mob concept she'd come up with that gave the entire campaign a fun, fresh and hip feel, and would showcase all of the resort's activities and focus on an entertaining matchmaking theme. The ad agency had the means to make the video a viral sensation that would sweep the internet and increase the resort's visibility, while appealing to singles looking for a fun and unique way to find romance, and ultimately, love.

Love. The one word prompted Chloe's heart to flutter wildly in her chest as she stared at Aiden, who was still deep in concentration as he typed away on his laptop computer, oblivious to anything but his campaign. Good God, had she done the unthinkable and fallen in love with Aiden? She swallowed hard in denial, but it was getting more and more difficult to dismiss the intense feelings he evoked that indicated she was perilously close to letting their brief island affair mess with her head and her emotions. And that had disaster written all over it for both of them.

They'd always been friends, and the sex between them had been nothing short of amazing, but spending the past week with him as an intimate couple had unlocked something inside of her that made her want…more. More time with Aiden, and not just between the sheets. And *that* was a huge revelation for her, considering she swore she'd never, ever, allow herself to be that vulnerable with another man again.

But there was no denying that she enjoyed being with Aiden. He made her laugh and he'd even pried some of her darkest memories out of her. She'd shared things with him she'd never intended to, let him into places she'd sealed off after her painful breakup with Neil—and that was something she'd never shared with anyone before.

But the fact remained, they were colleagues, working for a company with a strict no dating policy. She had goals for her future, and the promotion she wanted so badly was within her reach…yet a part of her wondered if she wanted it bad enough to walk away from Aiden after this week together. She gave her head a slight shake at how one-sided her thoughts were. While she and Aiden had had a great time together, he'd never given her any kind of indication that the two of them had a future beyond the resort. And even though she'd opened up about her past with him, he'd remained tight-lipped about his own divorce and what had transpired between him and his ex-wife. But he'd obviously been burned, and she was curious to know what had happened.

With a low groan, Aiden stretched his arms over his head and rolled his neck from side to side, easing the tension that had settled there. "I think I'm just about done."

"Me, too," she said, though there were a few things she needed to refine and tweak. But those could easily be done back at the office. "How did your presentation turn out?"

"Honestly, better than I'd anticipated," he said, a pleased note to his voice. "I just have a few more final touches to add, but I have to admit that Hattie is quite a convincing matchmaker."

Chloe knew he'd spent the past three days interviewing employees at the resort about the older woman's reputation, along with perusing dozens upon dozens of letters written from past guests about how accurate Hattie's predictions had been. Considering how the woman's skills directly related to the resort's main purpose of pairing up compatible singles, Hattie's expertise was hugely overlooked and underutilized. Especially from an advertising perspective.

"It's a fantastic marketing angle," she said, then took a long, cool drink from her bottled water.

"So is your flash mob concept." He leaned back in his chair and smiled indulgently. "It's very current and trendy."

"Thanks." Despite the fact that Perry had instructed them to develop individual campaigns,

Chloe appreciated that she and Aiden trusted each other enough to bounce ideas off one another to help refine their own strategies. He was incredibly creative and insightful, and she loved brainstorming with him.

"I guess it just depends on what the vice president is looking for and what appeals to him the most," she said of their individual ideas. "And we have no idea what the boys are doing, either."

They'd nicknamed the two executives with the Metro Ad Agency "the boys," even though they knew their names—Darryl and Ken. While she and Aiden had seen them around the resort, they hadn't fraternized with the enemy, and they'd been careful about keeping their own advertising concepts under wraps.

Aiden rubbed his thumb along his jaw, the brief hesitation glimmering in his gaze giving way to something more decisive. "Would you like to see my PowerPoint presentation? I'd really like to get your take on it."

Her eyes widened in surprise. Yes, they'd verbally discussed their campaigns over the past few days, but she hadn't expected him to share such an integral part of his presentation with her. It was such a huge show of trust on his part, and she was dying to see what he'd come up with.

"Yes, I'd love to."

He withdrew the small flash drive from the side of his laptop and slid it across the conference table to her. She connected the memory stick to her own computer, and within seconds the program streamed onto her monitor in a compilation of slides spotlighting some of the resort's most spectacular amenities, and featuring photographs of the tropical landscaping, gorgeous beaches and couples enjoying many of the recreational offerings.

The pictures that Ricardo had taken for Aiden conjured excitement and passion, and he'd used them in a way that was romantic and seductive. The presentation segued into a video interview with Hattie in her greenhouse. With a sparkle in her deep brown eyes, Hattie introduced herself as the island's resident matchmaker and spoke about seeing that magic spark between two people and knowing when a couple was meant to be together.

In another clip, upon Hattie's urging, a young man and woman gently grasped the stamen of that pink hybrid flower Chloe and Aiden had also touched. The stem turned a deep, dark crimson in both places, and with a satisfied smile Hattie pronounced them soul mates…if they opened up their hearts and *believed.*

Chloe believed, and that knowledge sent a crazy, unexpected surge of adrenaline rushing through her veins. She might have been doubtful about that flower and Hattie's prediction that first day in the greenhouse, but her shifting feelings for Aiden supported the older woman's claim that he could possibly be *the one* for her.

In her head, she could deny the inevitable all she

wanted, but in reality she knew it was too late. There was no stopping the emotions blossoming deep in her heart when it came to the man sitting across the table from her. It was a frightening realization, because she had no idea how he felt about her.

Aiden's presentation offered hope and romantic possibilities to singles wanting to fall in love, and the irony of Aiden's core message to his target audience wasn't lost on Chloe. He was hinging his campaign on Hattie and her matchmaking intuition, yet he clearly didn't really believe that the older woman had the ability to see a couple's fate. For him, Hattie was nothing more than an advertising tactic to romanticize the St. Raphael Resort and the island itself.

As a marketing ploy, it worked, and Chloe knew in her gut that between her flash mob idea and Aiden's more traditional approach, his packed an emotional punch that would be difficult for her to trump. Not that she wouldn't do everything in her power to sell her concept and give Aiden a fight to the finish. Being competitive was in her nature, and ultimately she wanted the St. Raphael account and the bonus that came with it.

"So, what do you think?"

Chloe didn't miss the anxious note to Aiden's voice, as if her opinion mattered to him. Glancing up from her monitor, she met his gaze and gave him the truth. "I think it's phenomenal."

The stiff set of his shoulders relaxed. "Really?"

She smiled. "Yes, really. But how is it that you and

your presentation made me believe in Hattie and the magic of this island when you have your doubts?"

"I'm creating a perception of the resort and engaging the consumer," he said with a nonchalant shrug. "That's what you and I do. I don't have to believe in the product in order to sell it. As long as it works for the resort and their matchmaking theme, that's all that matters."

His reply was logical and rational, and she couldn't argue his point. "You're right."

He stood up and began gathering the files and papers he'd spread out on his side of the conference table and tucked them into his leather attaché case. "There's a few things I need to follow up on before we leave the resort tomorrow, but we're still on for tonight, yes?"

More than anything, she wanted this last night with Aiden before their affair ended and they returned to real life. And she was feeling selfish enough not to want to share him with anyone, or anything. "Instead of attending the farewell gala, how about you come up to my room? We can order room service and have our own private party, just the two of us?"

His gaze heated, matching the slow, wicked smile on his lips as he added his laptop to his bag. "I like that idea. A lot. I'll come by around seven."

She honestly couldn't wait, and she planned to make the most of their final night together. She watched him walk out of the conference room, already planning in her mind how the evening would go.

It wasn't until she was finished working on her own campaign an hour later that she realized she still had his flash drive with his PowerPoint presentation. She tucked the small device into her briefcase to give to him later, and with the rest of her afternoon free, she decided to take advantage of the complimentary spa package the resort had extended to her when she'd first arrived.

AIDEN ARRIVED AT Chloe's room a few minutes before seven. As he stood in front of her closed door, he was struck with the somber realization that tonight was the end of their time together. Tomorrow was Sunday, and after nearly a week at the St. Raphael Resort, they were heading back to Boston and to real life…as colleagues, not lovers.

His gut twisted with a twinge of disappointment, because he knew that reverting back to being just friends and coworkers was going to be incredibly difficult to do—and it wasn't all about giving up their sexual encounters, though he was definitely going to miss that, too.

No, it had more to do with their comfortable conversations and how quickly and easily he could laugh with her. She made him feel lighter inside than he had in years…and she also made him realize all the things he wanted in his life. Marriage. A family. A wife who shared his same life goals. He wished

Chloe could be that woman, but there was no possible way.

As much as he and Chloe clicked, intellectually and physically, they had no future together. Their goals were on the opposite end of the spectrum. She was career-focused and competitive, and while he admired her drive and determination, all that ambition was a sharp reminder of just how far his ex-wife had gone to achieve her own personal success. Though he no longer believed Chloe would betray him like his ex had, their future desires were incompatible and out of sync.

He exhaled a deep breath and knocked on the door. No matter how hard he tried, he couldn't keep his past out of the equation when looking at his future. So, he'd made sure his heart and emotions were kept out of this affair. It didn't matter that the resident matchmaker had deemed them soul mates, or that a silly flower had backed up Hattie's claim, because he was pragmatic and realistic enough to know that compatibility went much deeper than just sexual chemistry.

Those thoughts quickly fled his mind as the door swung open and Chloe filled the frame, happy to see him, a soft pink flush on her cheeks and the green glow in her hazel eyes outshining the gold and brown. Her peach-colored halter-style dress exposed a lot of smooth, sun-kissed skin that tempted him to touch and caress. She'd left her hair down, falling around her shoulders in those soft, careless waves that told him she'd let her hair dry naturally, instead of blow-drying the silky strands straight. She wore minimal makeup, just a sweep of black on her lashes and a glossy shine on her lips, and he loved this "au natural" look on her.

"I hope you're hungry," she said with a welcoming smile.

Her comment, rife with unintentional innuendo, fed into the need for her that seemed to suddenly consume Aiden. "I'm famished," he murmured as he stepped into her room and kicked the door shut.

Her eyes widened as he pressed her up against the nearest wall and dropped his mouth to hers, devouring her as if he was a starving man and she, his last meal. That's certainly what tonight felt like to him, and he couldn't stop the desperate urge to gorge himself on Chloe in hopes of satisfying that overwhelming need he felt for her.

But as he deepened the kiss and her mouth softened beneath the wild, reckless onslaught of his, the longing inside of him grew stronger, making him feel as though he'd never get enough of this woman, no matter how many times he had her.

He was so lost in the heated desire coursing through him that it took him a moment to realize that Chloe had placed a hand on his chest and was giving him a gentle push to end the kiss. Reluctantly, he lifted his head and stared down at her. They were both breathing hard, and he wasn't sure what to make of her putting a stop to something that clearly could have ended with them both naked and him buried deep inside of her. He knew his thoughts were selfish and reckless, but if this was their last night together, he wanted to make sure they made the most of it.

Chloe ran her tongue along her bottom lip, then smiled up at him. "That was a nice hello, but how about we save the rest of that for dessert?" she suggested huskily. "I went ahead and ordered dinner for both of us, and it's already been delivered. It's going to get cold if we don't get started. Besides, the sun is just beginning to set and I don't want to miss that, either."

Before he could reply, she clasped his hand in hers and pulled him toward the sliding glass doors leading to her balcony, giving him a chance to gather some semblance of control and calm his raging emotions. A small table had been set up for the two of them, with a white tablecloth, silverware and crystal glasses for the bottle of wine she'd ordered. Their dinner was covered with silver domes to keep the contents warm, and they had a spectacular view of the bright orange sun as it slowly lowered itself beyond the horizon.

He sat down next to her and relaxed in his seat, inhaling the scent of jasmine—the island's signature scent. He heard calypso music playing somewhere in the distance, and guessed it was probably drifting from the farewell party. Their dinner was intimate and private, yet still allowed them to enjoy many of the resort's romantic nuances.

"I hope you like chicken primavera," she said as they both removed the cover from their dishes and set them aside.

As soon as the savory scent of creamy garlic basil sauce filled his senses, his stomach rumbled, loud enough for Chloe to hear. She laughed and he grinned.

"I guess I'm hungrier for *food* than I thought."

"Good, because I'm starving," she admitted, smoothing her cloth napkin on her lap.

He reached for the bottle of wine and poured them each a glass of the chilled Pinot Grigio, a nice pairing for the pasta. They ate in silence for a few minutes, enjoying the island atmosphere just beyond the balcony, as well as the stunning sunset dipping lower and lower where the ocean met the skyline.

"So, tell me something about yourself that I don't already know," Chloe said after a while, her tone light and casual. "Something that might surprise me."

He knew she was just being conversational, but her personal question struck a chord in him, because the things she didn't know about him were private incidences in his life that he'd normally only share with someone he trusted or had a connection with.

And Chloe, he realized, was both.

He ate a bite of his pasta as he mulled over what he wanted to share with her before deciding to give her some insight into how he'd shunned family expectations to follow his own career path. "I'm the first son in three generations who bucked tradition of getting a job in law enforcement."

"Really?" Her brows lifted in genuine surprise. "I just can't imagine you as a cop. Was your family upset?"

"My mother understood because I was always the creative one with these big ideas, but my father was disappointed in my choice to major in advertising and marketing in college. My grandfather was a cop, then my dad. He was this tough military guy who just assumed that both of his boys would follow in his footsteps." Aiden absently swirled his wine in his glass. "At least my brother continued the proud family tradition, and while my father and brother still give me a hard time about being the black sheep of the family, it's all in good humor."

Her eyes glimmered with amusement, and she tipped her head curiously. "Does your brother at least enjoy being a police officer?"

"He did," Aiden said, then seeing the questions in her gaze, he explained, "A few years ago Sam was shot on the job, and the injury made him reassess what he wanted to do. Now he's a private investigator with his own business, so while he's technically self-employed, he still has some involvement with law enforcement."

She pushed her pasta and chicken around on her plate, then found a carrot and stabbed it with her fork to eat. "He seems like a nice guy."

"*Nice* is being generous," he said, though there

was a rumble of affection in his voice for his brother. "Mostly, he's a pain in the ass."

"I suppose siblings can be a pain sometimes," she said softly, and drained the rest of the wine from her glass.

He heard the wistful note in her voice, reminding him that she was an only child, with a mother who hadn't been an ideal parent. "It's your turn to tell me something I don't already know about you," he said, refilling her glass with more Pinot Grigio and topping off his own.

She leaned forward and whispered mischievously, "I love reading romance novels. The hotter and sexier they are, the better. It's like mind candy after a long day at the office."

Her sexy secret definitely intrigued him, because he would have pegged her for a straight literary fiction kind of girl. "So, you like books with hot sex and a happily-ever-afters?"

She shrugged and placed her fork on her plate, finished with her meal. "It's nice to believe that it's possible."

"You don't?"

A small smile touched her lips. "Well, considering my mother's track record, and my own with Neil, I think I'm better off making my own happiness."

Despite her past experience, he wanted to give her something to believe in. "My parents are still married after thirty-five years, so it's definitely possible."

"And you're divorced."

Her words were direct and to the point, leaving him little choice but to address her statement. "That doesn't mean I don't think I could be happy and settled with someone else who has the same goals and ideals that I do."

She relaxed back in her chair, her eyes meeting his for a moment over the rim of her wineglass as she took a drink. "Was that the problem between you and your ex-wife?" she asked, digging a little deeper. "Incompatibility?"

Aiden had managed to avoid this particular conversation with Chloe numerous times, and he was tempted to evade the discussion now. His marriage and divorce wasn't something he liked to talk about, with anyone, but she'd shared so much with him this past week, he felt compelled to do the same now. And maybe, by getting his own past out in the open it would help to serve as a reminder of why things with Chloe could never work out beyond this temporary affair.

"Paige and I actually had a lot in common," he said, trying to sound nonchalant, even though he knew this conversation was going to dredge up emotions he'd rather not relive. "On the surface, we enjoyed the same things, and had the same interests. She was a defense attorney, so we both had careers in the corporate world that required drive and ambition to succeed. But I never had a clue just how cutthroat she really was."

He rubbed a hand along his jaw, feeling a familiar tension twist through him. "Before we got married, we talked about having a family, and we both agreed we wanted kids after a year or so. But every time I brought up the subject of having a baby, she said she wasn't ready because her career was really starting to take off. I understood and backed off, but when one year turned into two and she claimed she still wasn't ready to have a baby, the issue became a huge source of contention between us."

"I could imagine," Chloe said softly, as if she truly sympathized with the situation. And him.

"The more we fought, the colder and more distant Paige became," he went on, hating this next part but forcing himself to tell her the entire story, no matter how difficult. "Then one day I came home from work and she was already in bed and claimed she wasn't feeling well, but I could tell something was off. Paige was *never* sick. Yet, she'd been fine that morning when we each went to work. I decided to go and get her some soup from a nearby deli, and since it was more convenient to drive her car than mine, I went to grab her keys from her purse and saw this piece of paper with a local hospital logo across the top. I was both curious and concerned, so I read the paperwork and discovered it was instructions for aftercare for a surgical abortion procedure she'd had that afternoon. She'd terminated our baby without ever telling me she was pregnant."

Chloe gasped, her eyes round in shock. "Aiden,

I'm so sorry," she whispered, obviously stunned and appalled by what he'd revealed.

His hand curled into a fist on the table, but he managed to tamp down the bitterness threatening to engulf him. He could recall that moment so vividly, how everything inside him had gone stone cold and yet he'd wanted so desperately to believe that there was some kind of logical explanation for what he'd discovered…for what Paige had done.

Instead, he'd been slapped with the truth of just how little she valued their marriage, and the lengths she'd gone to protect and secure her climb up the corporate ladder. She might as well have stabbed him directly in the heart with a sharp knife; the pain of her deceit had been that enormous and great.

"I confronted Paige, and she didn't even deny it," he said with a harsh laugh that made his chest hurt. "She just calmly told me that the pregnancy was a mistake and she wasn't willing to give up her job to take care of a baby she didn't want. It didn't matter to her what I might have wanted. She gave me no choice in the matter."

Chloe reached across the table and placed her hand over his fisted one, her thumb grazing across his knuckles in a soothing caress. "That was an incredibly selfish thing for her to do."

He met her gaze, seeing the compassion etching her features. He could feel her empathy for what he'd gone through, and her sensitive, supportive response played tug-of-war with his own emotions and made him see her in a different light, too. One week with Chloe, without any outside influences to dictate their feelings, and she was becoming a woman who knew him better than anyone else in recent years.

She stood up, pushed the small table out of the way, and then sat down on his lap, the move more comforting than sexual. He welcomed the tenderness she offered, which was something that had been missing in his life for much too long.

She pressed her warm palm against his cheek, so sweet and caring. "I can't begin to imagine how difficult it was for you to find out about the abortion after the fact. You deserved better than that."

He shook his head, a part of him still mired in the past. "How could I be so wrong about someone—someone I actually married?" It was a question he knew he'd never have the answer to, but it haunted him, nonetheless. "How could the one person I trusted so unconditionally betray me in a way I never thought possible, all because her career was more important than our marriage?"

"You couldn't have known what she'd do, and she should have been open and honest with you, instead of stringing you along with false hopes."

Despite his own bitterness, Aiden realized just how similar their past situations were, more than he ever would have expected. How Neil had presented one persona to Chloe, then revealed another after time. The same as Paige.

She dipped her head and settled her lips on his,

the touch soft and reverent. A healing balm to his fractured soul. He accepted the kiss, wanting it, craving her in ways that went beyond pure physical desire and shook him to the core, making him think about the reasons why he believed things could never work between him and Chloe. Made him wonder how something so wrong could feel so damn right.

His confusion gave way to heated passion as their mouths fused more deeply, and that wild desperation rose within him again. An impatience to have her, to lose himself so completely in her lush body that only the two of them existed, and nothing else. The need to make this one final night together last as long as possible.

Abruptly, he stood up with her in his arms and carried her back into the hotel room. Next to the bed, he set her down on her feet, still kissing her, his hands sliding around to the nape of her neck to untie the bow holding up the top panels of her halter dress. The fabric fell away, and he immediately filled his hands with her breasts, groaning into her mouth as her nipples puckered tight and hard against his palms.

She moaned, too, her fingers slipping beneath his T-shirt to stroke his bare skin, to skim her thumbs across his own rigid nipples while she nibbled on his bottom lip. He pushed the rest of her dress over her hips and let it fall to the floor. She tugged his shirt over his head and tossed it aside.

More languid kisses and sultry caresses ensued as

they finished undressing one another, much too leisurely for his liking. But every time he tried to speed things up a few notches, she deliberately slowed him down, making him excruciatingly aware of the fact that tonight was going to be much, much different than all the other nights before.

It was so unlike Chloe to want to take her time—she who always wanted to be in control, to have the upper hand, who opted for hard and fast over soft and slow and thorough. But as he followed her down onto the bed, donned a condom, then moved over her, he couldn't help but note the subtle change in the back of his mind and knew exactly what this joining was.

They were making love.

Tonight, there was no hiding behind forbidden fantasies, wild seductions or frenzied, reckless mating. The emotion between them was palpable, and it made him feel raw and exposed. Made his heart feel wide-open and vulnerable.

Fairly certain that he'd fallen in love with her, he swallowed hard and tried to maintain his composure. With her soft, giving body pinned beneath his, the hard length of his cock nestled between her spread thighs and his hands framing her face, he saw the longing in her gaze and knew with absolute certainty that their no strings affair had suddenly become very complicated. Despite the revelation, he lacked the willpower necessary to stop whatever was happening between them, regardless of his own fears and misgivings. He wasn't sure he even wanted to, because he didn't know how he was going to live without this, without *her* in his life.

As if sensing his emotional turmoil, she wrapped her slender legs around his waist and urged his hips forward, distracting him with the slick heat of her desire drenching the sensitive head of his dick.

She arched beneath him, restlessly rubbing her breasts against his chest. "Take me, Aiden," she whispered.

Temptation and heaven beckoned, and with a long, grinding flex of his hips he slid all the way home… impossibly, deliciously deep. A perfect fit, she clasped him tight, and as he withdrew then pushed back in, those internal muscles contracted and her soft moan became a whimper of need.

He breathed her name before he claimed her mouth, taking the kiss deeper with a purposeful slide of his tongue. His hips began pumping and grinding against hers, filling her, over and over. He took her with mindless greed, with heat and passion and selfish demand, and knew by the way her body strained against the onslaught of his that he was giving her as much pleasure as he was taking.

She turned wild beneath him, her hips rising to meet each of his heavy, driving thrusts. Her hands gripped his muscled back, holding on to him as she started quivering around his cock, the exquisite sensation more than he could bear. The rolling waves of her release milked his shaft, and he could no longer hold back.

His orgasm slammed into him, exploding out of control, and he came so long and hard he saw stars. And in that moment, he surrendered everything to her…possibly even his heart and soul.

10

AIDEN WOKE JUST before five in the morning, still in Chloe's bed, his body spooning the back of hers and his arm wrapped around her waist. The realization that he was still there when he should have been long gone jolted him to full consciousness.

After their first night together, as if by unspoken agreement, neither one of them had stayed the entire night in the other's bed…and now he understood why. Because sharing this kind of intimacy was a dangerous thing and made their relationship feel *real,* when their affair was only supposed to be a temporary fling.

But last night he hadn't been able to get enough of Chloe, and every time he started to go, she would lure him right back in with a seductive kiss, a whispered promise or an erotic caress…until they were both too exhausted to do anything but fall into a deep, sated sleep together.

Which brought him back around to his current

predicament. He couldn't resist Chloe, that much was clear. But his desire for her went beyond the physical. Everything about her felt good and right, in ways he never would have imagined. She exhilarated him, challenged him in ways he enjoyed, and made him want to open himself up to the possibility of more. With her. Despite her drive and ambition and need to climb the corporate ladder.

Because he was falling in love with her.

The thought terrified him, and it was that tangle of fear currently tightening his chest that had him itching to get out while the getting was still good.

He couldn't stay. He had to leave. Not just Chloe, but the island, too. There were so many conflicting feelings battling within him, and he wasn't ready to face Chloe until he sorted things out in his own head. And the only way he could do that was to put distance between them. He had decisions he needed to make, and none of them were easy. But he just couldn't think straight when he was around her.

Ignoring the dull ache in his chest, he eased away from the delicious warmth of her body. She let out a soft sigh and snuggled into the warm spot he'd left behind, giving him the opportunity to move off the bed. Careful not to awaken her, he quietly got dressed, knowing he was taking the coward's way out, but unable to change what he needed to do…for his own self-preservation.

They were supposed to leave the island today, anyways. He was just taking the very early morning flight out, instead of waiting around for the late afternoon one they'd initially booked. He had everything he needed for his campaign, so there was no reason to stay, and he'd be long gone before she realized what he'd done.

Finding the standard hotel notepad and pen on her nightstand, he wrote her a quick note letting her know he'd flown out early, and that he'd see her back in the office on Monday morning. Then, with one last longing look at her, he silently slipped out of her room and hoped like hell he wasn't walking away from the best thing that had ever happened to him.

CHLOE WASN'T SURPRISED to wake up alone, but as she reread the vague, impersonal note that Aiden had left for her to find, a huge knot of hurt and disappointment twisted inside her stomach. He'd decided to leave the island earlier than their scheduled afternoon flight, and considering it was after eight in the morning, he was likely already gone.

She set the piece of paper back on the nightstand and dragged her fingers through her disheveled hair, reminding herself that no promises had been made between them other than to indulge in a hot affair during their time at the resort.

And today definitely marked *the end,* no matter how much she wished otherwise.

A foolish part of her had hoped that after last night's discussion about his ex-wife, she and Aiden had forged an intimate bond that went deeper than just appeasing their lust for one another. And the way he'd made love to her after sharing something so painful, there had been no denying the emotion and need pouring from him.

Last night had been so different from all the other times they'd been together. When she finally fell asleep, curled up against Aiden, safe and secure in his arms, she'd truly believed that something significant had changed between them. That despite their differences and the standing no dating policy at the firm, that they could quietly continue seeing each other outside of work and find out if what they'd started here on the island translated into a real-world relationship.

But she realized it was all wishful thinking on her part. If Aiden's actions were any indication, he had no desire to continue *anything* with her...and that realization hurt more than she wanted to admit.

She pulled in a deep breath, and the lingering scent of Aiden filled her senses. Refusing to sit in her room for the rest of the morning wallowing in what could have been, she decided she needed to get out, to breathe fresh air and clear her head.

She took a quick shower, changed into a lightweight sundress and sandals, and headed down to the lobby, which was filled with guests going through the check-out process, and groups of people saying farewell to the friends they'd made. There was laughter and lively conversations, as well as many couples walking hand in hand, giving credence to the fact that love matches had been made, and would hopefully flourish even long after they left the St. Raphael resort.

Feeling a twinge of jealousy for those who were heading back home in love and with the promise of a bright, fresh future with someone they'd met, Chloe quickly made her way outside, where it was a beautiful, sunny, breezy day. She walked aimlessly along various pathways, inhaling the familiar fragrance of jasmine, until she realized she'd ended up at the island greenhouses. The flowers beckoned to her, and she didn't hesitate to enter the glass enclosure.

Silence greeted Chloe, along with the perfumed scent of all the tropical flowers growing around her. She was immediately reminded of the first time she'd been in here, with Aiden, and when she caught sight of those fuchsia flowers that Hattie claimed to predict a couple's compatibility, she slowly strolled over to those potted plants and lightly stroked one of the soft, velvety petals.

"Hi there," a familiar female voice said from behind Chloe. "I wasn't expecting anyone to stop by the greenhouse today, not with everyone leaving the island."

Chloe turned around, and as soon as she met Hattie's perceptive gaze, she realized why she'd come here...even if it had been subconsciously. Because she believed Hattie's claim, that the possibility existed that she and Aiden could be soul mates—even if Aiden didn't. Chloe felt the connection in her heart, and other places she'd thought she'd closed off after the way things ended with Neil.

"I was just taking a walk around the area and ended up here," she said easily. "Did you have a busy week here in the greenhouse?"

"Actually, I did. A lot of matchmaking going on, that's for sure," she said with a throaty laugh, then she tipped her head, regarding Chloe a bit more speculatively. "Where is your man? The one so interested in my matchmaking skills, yet so skeptical about love, even when it's right in front of him?"

There Hattie went again, spouting insight about a person. But as far as Aiden was concerned, Chloe had to admit the other woman's intuition was pretty dead-on. "Aiden took the early morning flight out," she said, keeping her reply simple, when it was anything but.

Hattie gently took Chloe's hand between the two of hers, her deep brown eyes kind and tender. "He left you," she said softly, knowingly.

"Yes," Chloe whispered, hating the way her throat closed up with emotion.

"The man is a fool," Hattie said with a scowl that made Chloe chuckle, before the older woman grew serious once again. "But he's also been betrayed in the past and doesn't trust easily. You've been hurt, too. But you, at least, are open to love again."

Hattie's statement was very matter-of-fact, and Chloe no longer questioned how the woman knew such things, especially since what she'd just said was dead-on—about both her *and* Aiden. It was true that the way things ended between her and Neil had left her guarded and more intent on exerting her time and energy on her career, rather than another man. After Neil had taken control of so many aspects of her life and decisions, she'd sworn she'd never give another man that much influence over her.

But with Aiden, there was no emotional power-play between them, just an equal give and take that had turned their flirtatious friendship into something much deeper and caring. This past week with Aiden had made her realize just how much she missed being in a real relationship…one based on mutual respect, caring, great sex and the kind of faith that came in knowing that Aiden would never do anything to deliberately hurt her.

There was no question that her heart ached for Aiden and what he'd gone through with his ex-wife. They both had screwed-up pasts, things that had happened to each of them that kept them from letting someone close again. But after everything they'd shared, she trusted Aiden, and that's what ultimately mattered.

Unfortunately, those feelings weren't reciprocated.

The thought made her chest hurt. "I am open to love again, but that doesn't do me much good when the man I want isn't."

Hattie gave the back of her hand a consoling pat. "You need to give him a little push, I think," she said thoughtfully. "If you haven't told him how you feel, then you need to. Men can be very obtuse that way."

The other woman managed to make Chloe laugh, but her biggest fear was that she'd put her feelings for Aiden out in the open, and he'd reject them. But then again, when had she ever backed down from something she believed in? "No guts, no glory, huh?"

"Yes, you strike me as a woman with a lot of guts," Hattie said, her tone amused. "The worst thing in life is living with regrets. Don't let your man be one of them."

"Thank you," Chloe said, and gave Hattie a hug, because this woman had given her more useful advice in the span of fifteen minutes than her own mother ever had.

Filled with a renewed purpose, she headed back to the resort, wanting to believe that Aiden's reasons for bolting on her were *because* of the emotional impact of what had happened between them. But she wouldn't know for sure, not until she had the chance to ask him herself. Because unlike him, she needed closure to this affair, one way or another. She wanted to look into his eyes, tell him what was in her heart, and know that she'd laid herself bare, with no regrets.

As she made her way into the hotel lobby, she caught sight of Darryl and Ken, the Metro Ad Agency boys, who were talking with Edward Luca, the vice president of St. Raphael Resort. She could tell by their expressions that it wasn't a casual conversation, but rather a more intense discussion that raised her awareness and business instincts. They'd all had their time with Luca during the week to discuss the resort and potential ideas. They weren't supposed to pitch their presentations until next week, after they'd returned to their respective ad agencies to refine their campaigns.

There was just something about how insistent Ken was being with Luca that didn't sit right with Chloe. Curious to know what they were discussing, she stopped at a nearby rack of brochures about the island, and with her back to the trio she perused the selection while blatantly eavesdropping.

"We really feel we have the winning campaign for the St. Raphael Resort, and we're ready to pitch our presentation today, before we leave the island," Ken said, doing his best to convince the VP to give them an edge over the competition, without outright saying so.

It was all Chloe could do to keep her mouth shut, when she wanted to step in and argue just whose campaign was superior. She'd never be so crass in front of the vice president of the resort, but that didn't mean she wasn't going to make damn sure that she and Aiden had their shot, too.

"I have meetings with your agency, as well as Perry & Associates next week," Edward said hesitantly. "I wasn't planning on viewing anyone's campaign here on the island."

"We understand," Darryl chimed in, his tone a

bit more assertive. "But we feel that our presentation is all you need to see to make a final decision."

The man's gall and arrogance made Chloe's blood boil in her veins, and she nearly tore the brochure she held in her hands in half. Maintaining her composure took extreme effort.

"That's very presumptuous of you both," Luca said, his tone frank.

"We're just confident."

There was a distinct pause, then Edward spoke again. "All right," he said, a twinge of reluctance in his voice. "Let's set up a meeting in conference room C in half an hour, and I'll see what you've come up with."

"Excellent," Ken said in a too cocky tone. "We'll be there."

As the three of them went their separate ways, Chloe swallowed back her anger and knew she had no choice but to be present at that meeting, too. Because there was no way she was going to let those boys steal something that rightfully belonged to her or Aiden.

AFTER BOARDING A small puddle jumper plane from the island early that morning, Aiden sat in the Nassau, Bahamas, airport, waiting to catch his connecting flight to Boston. He had a little less than two hours to kill, and way too much time alone to *think.* About Chloe, and the way he'd slipped out on her this morning.

At the time, it had been a defensive reaction, a way to protect himself from having to deal with the intense emotions rioting within him. True, those feelings were still present and wreaking havoc with every rational reason he tried to come up with why things would never work between him and Chloe, so why did he think that any amount of distance was going to change that?

He dragged his hands through his hair, his stomach roiling with a ton of regrets, because he could only imagine how Chloe had felt when she'd realized he'd left without so much as a goodbye, or an explanation. Just a brusque note, when she deserved better than an impersonal brush-off.

Jesus, he was such an ass, and Aiden was certain his brother Sam would heartily agree with that sentiment. If he could turn back the clock and do things differently, he would, but trapped between the island and Boston while waiting for his flight, without any cell service to the island, there was nothing he could do about his stupidity.

Knowing he had no choice but to wait and deal with Chloe and the situation until they were both back in Boston, he decided he needed to keep himself distracted, or let his thoughts drive him crazy. Deciding to use his idle time to refine his presentation, he retrieved his computer from his leather attaché. While his laptop booted up, he reached into the front pocket of his briefcase for the flash drive with his PowerPoint presentation, but it wasn't there.

Frowning, he thought back to when he last remembered having it, and his stomach churned with apprehension when he realized he'd never gotten it back from Chloe.

He didn't believe she'd deliberately kept it from him, and it wasn't as though he didn't have a backup on his laptop's hard drive, but he couldn't stop the niggle of unease coursing through him. He knew how much securing this campaign meant to her—just as much as it meant to him, and he wanted to trust her but…

He shook his head of those negative, cynical thoughts before they could completely form. She'd never do that to him. Then again, hadn't he thought the same of his ex-wife?

No. He wasn't going to go there. He had to believe she wouldn't betray him that way. Besides, what was Chloe going to do with his presentation in a day's time? They were due in the office tomorrow morning, and he'd get the flash drive back then. No harm. No foul.

HEART PUMPING WITH adrenaline, Chloe rushed back to her hotel room, knowing she had a limited amount of time to change into something more professional than her casual sundress, and gather up what she needed to give Edward Luca the best, most cohesive presentation possible with such short notice. Most of her concept was laid out, but she still hadn't come up with a catchy tagline that the resort could use in their advertising and branding. She thought she'd have more time to figure out a slogan, but she was just going to have to wing it. It certainly wouldn't be the first time for that.

Feeling frantic because the clock was ticking, she found a simple black dress that she hadn't worn yet and hastily slipped it on, and added a pair of red pumps. The pop of color gave her a boost of confidence, yet kept her overall appearance classy and sophisticated. Quickly, she pulled her hair into a sleek ponytail, then focused on the material she needed to take with her for this very impromptu meeting.

As she fired up her laptop to make sure that her PowerPoint slides were as clean as possible, she couldn't stop the frustration making its way to the surface. God, she wished that Aiden was still here on the island, that he hadn't left on the morning flight out. Even though they had separate campaigns and ideas to offer, this was something they should be doing *together,* but he'd left her with no choice but to go it alone.

Then she remembered she still had his flash drive with his matchmaking concept on it and experienced a swell of relief. If Aiden couldn't be here, at least she'd be able to pitch his presentation, too, and that's all that mattered—that the two of them got a fair shot at the campaign.

She gathered up her laptop and retrieved Aiden's flash drive and made her way down to conference room C. The door was already closed, and she heard male voices from inside, indicating that the boys were already presenting their campaign ideas to Luca.

She paced the carpeted floor in the hallway, tension tightening across her chest. She didn't usually get nervous before a meeting, but she and Aiden each had so much riding on this deal. She didn't want to blow it for either one of them. Knowing she had to shake off her anxiety, and fast, she leaned back against the nearest wall, closed her eyes, and took the Zen approach. She inhaled deep, tranquil breaths, until a peaceful calm cleared her mind and relaxed her body.

She could do this, she told herself, feeling more in control and focused. She loved to pitch to clients, and she was damn good at it. Today would be no different.

After a short while the door opened, and Edward's voice drifted out into the hallway as he spoke, "I do have to say, your advertising and marketing ideas are solid." Chloe smiled to herself, knowing she and Aiden were still in the game.

She'd been an ad executive long enough to know when a client used a bland word like *solid* to describe a marketing approach, they were being more diplomatic than complimentary. Edward hadn't been all that impressed by what he'd seen. If he had used terms such as unique or innovative, Chloe might have had a cause for concern, but his lack of any obvious enthusiasm filled her with a much needed surge of confidence.

Darryl and Ken strolled out of the room first, both of them wearing smug expressions…until they saw her standing there in the hallway, her laptop tucked under her arm, ready to present her campaign, too. She wanted to laugh at the shocked, *oh shit* looks on their faces, but managed to maintain her composure.

"Darryl. Ken," she acknowledged politely. "Mr. Luca, I'd also like the chance to pitch our company's campaign ideas today."

Edward arched a brow, amusement in his eyes. "By all means, come inside," he said, motioning for her to enter the conference room.

She walked inside, and he closed the door securely after her, watching as she set her laptop on the table and turned it on. He was dressed casually in a pair of khaki pants and a collared shirt, and she had to admit that for a man in his late fifties he was very good-looking. His hair was still thick and dark, though there was some silver at the temples that gave him a distinguished appearance. His body was still trim, his skin tanned, and there was a charm about him that put her at ease.

"You came prepared." He sat down in a nearby chair, then tipped his head curiously. "How did you know that the other agency was presenting their campaign?"

"I overheard them speaking with you down in the lobby, being more than a little insistent about pitching their presentation to you today," she replied honestly as she prepared her PowerPoint slides. "I wasn't about to leave the island without you seeing our campaign ideas, too."

He leaned back in his seat, admiration flickering in his gaze. "I have a lot of respect for a woman with such determination and fortitude."

She accepted his praise with a smile. "Oh, I have plenty of that, Mr. Luca."

"Where is Aiden?" Edward asked. "Shouldn't he be here, as well?"

Yes, he should have been there, but she'd never throw her partner under the bus for her own personal gain. Yes, she wanted this account badly, but she just didn't operate that way. She'd cover for him the best she could. "He had to leave the island early this morning."

"I hope everything is okay?" Edward asked, clearly concerned.

"Yes, everything is fine." She didn't offer details, because they weren't necessary. Besides, she wasn't about to share the real reason why Aiden had left… *her*. "In fact, I have his presentation with me, which is a different concept than my own, so I'm all set."

Edward gave an approving nod. "Excellent. Let's see what you've come up with."

She remained standing and positioned the laptop so that it faced Edward, but she could see the screen, as well, and control the speed of the slide show as she added her commentary to the presentation. She clicked the start button, and the program began to play.

As the slides clicked from one to the other, providing Edward with visual pictures of the resort, the island, the romantic aspects and her fun, sexy flash mob concept that conveyed personality and attitude, she explained the marketing strategies she had in mind, how she could boost their consumer visibility, and finished off her presentation with a memorable hook that would leave Edward wanting more.

"This campaign is all about finding love in paradise," she said, and realized that she'd just discovered her tagline for the St. Raphael Resort. Even she was proof that it was possible, considering she'd fallen in love with Aiden, and she latched on to the slogan.

"Find Love in Paradise," she said again as the slide show ended, this time giving the words more meaning and emotion, which was easy to do, since they came from her heart. "*That's* what your guests can expect when they arrive at St. Raphael."

Edward nodded thoughtfully. "I like it. It's very current and contemporary, but still stays true to the St. Raphael goal of making sure that everyone finds love…in paradise," he said, as if testing the slogan she'd come up with. He smiled, his eyes alight with enthusiasm, and she knew she'd definitely captivated him with her ideas.

She plugged in Aiden's flash drive and switched out her slide show for his, and continued the presentation with seamless ease. "The flash mob concept is certainly more modern, but Aiden has taken a more traditional approach with his campaign. Guests are still exposed to many romantic elements, but the one thing you could use as a draw is Hattie, your island matchmaker."

He frowned in confusion. "Hattie? She's just an old woman who enjoys tending to her exotic flowers and visiting with the guests."

The man had no idea just how valuable Hattie was to him, and the resort, and Chloe planned to enlighten him. "Oh, she's much more than that, Mr. Luca. She comes from a long line of matchmakers, and she's an untapped source that could elevate this resort's reputation. Take a look at this interview Aiden did with Hattie, and imagine the element of fantasy, romance and magic she could add to your campaign and advertising."

She clicked the play button, and the interview streamed onto the computer. Edward watched the video with interest, and she could tell by the surprised look on his face that he was seeing Hattie's potential, and all the ways they could utilize her as a draw to the island and resort.

As soon as the interview ended, she wrapped up the presentation with her closing statement. "Who else in this industry has an island matchmaker? Someone who intuitively knows if two people belong together and has a very high success rate of pairing up compatible couples, and uses an exotic flower to predict a couple's fate? No one. And that gives you, and the St. Raphael resort, a competitive edge."

He nodded in agreement. "It certainly does."

She exhaled a deep breath, knowing she'd given her absolute best, to both campaigns. "So, there you go...an exciting, fun flash mob, or a traditional matchmaker. The choice is yours."

"Both concepts are unique and innovative," he said, making Chloe smile by his choice of words, which were music to her ears. "You've made it very difficult to choose just one."

"Then I've done my job well," she said as she powered down her laptop. She knew Edward wouldn't give her an answer before she left, but she was confident that she'd engaged and captivated him more than the Metro boys had.

Now it was just a matter of which campaign Edward liked better...hers, or Aiden's?

11

AIDEN HAD BEEN home from the airport for a few hours and had just finished his last load of laundry when his cell phone rang. He glanced at the display, surprised to see his boss's cell number, especially since it was Sunday evening and Aiden was due back in the office in the morning.

He connected the call and answered. "Hey, Perry."

"Aiden," the older man said. "I just got a call from Edward Luca, the VP of the St. Raphael Resort. He told me that you had to leave the island early this morning. Is everything okay?"

Aiden inwardly cringed. Perry sounded more concerned than upset that he'd taken an earlier flight out, instead of the scheduled afternoon one, but Aiden wasn't about to tell his boss the real reason why. "I had everything I needed for my campaign, and I had a family situation that needed my attention." The little white lie was better than the truth...that he'd fallen in love with Chloe and didn't know how to handle his feelings for her. God, he was pathetic.

"Well, I just heard from Luca," Perry informed him enthusiastically. "Chloe pitched this brilliant concept this morning that would utilize a traditional matchmaker they have on the island. Luca loved the concept and is going with it!"

Perry went on, but the sudden ringing in Aiden's ears prevented him from hearing anything else. His stomach churned, making him ill, and his head began to spin. Angry thoughts flashed through his mind, fast and furious. Chloe had pitched without him and behind his back? And Jesus, she'd actually used his concept to win over Luca and secure the account? Used it as her own idea and took credit for something he'd created?

He pinched the bridge of his nose with his fingers, trying to see things another way, to think maybe he was wrong. But Perry himself had said, *Chloe pitched a brilliant concept using a traditional island matchmaker.* There was no other explanation.

How could a woman he thought he knew so well, a woman he'd trusted in so many ways, do something so unforgiveable? And how stupid was he for believing she was any different than Paige when it came to her career when he'd known all along how important climbing the corporate ladder was to Chloe?

After everything they'd shared, her betrayal cut deeper and sharper than a knife, and left him reeling with disbelief...yet there was no denying what Perry had just told him.

He shook his head hard, and forced himself to focus on what Perry was saying.

"...I haven't had the chance to talk to Chloe yet," his boss continued. "Luca told me that she missed the afternoon flight out because she'd been doing the presentation. He flew her out by private commuter plane, but chances are she missed her connecting flight in Nassau. I'll just see the two of you in the office in the morning."

"Uh, yeah, sure," Aiden said, because he didn't know what else to say. Besides, he was still trying to process the fact that Chloe had double-crossed him.

He disconnected the call and tossed his cell phone onto the counter. Frustration roiled through him. With no way to confront Chloe when she wasn't back in Boston yet, his anger simmered all night long. By the time he arrived at the office in the morning, he was like a lit fuse waiting to explode.

AFTER ONLY A few hours of sleep in her own bed, Chloe's alarm clock startled her awake. It took everything in her not to hit the snooze button and go back to sleep. Instead she dragged her tired body into the shower. Exhausted or not after her flight snafu yesterday that had finally gotten her back to Boston after midnight, she was expected in the office this morning.

She hadn't had a chance to call Aiden, or talk to

Perry about her spontaneous meeting yesterday with Edward Luca, and she needed to let them both know that she'd already pitched their ideas, and why. She still felt it had been the right thing to do, because there was no way she wanted the Metro boys to have any kind of leverage over her or Aiden.

A hot shower helped to clear her head, but she couldn't shake the fatigue and jet lag weighing her down. She figured it would probably take a day or so for her body to readjust. Dressed in a leopard print A-line skirt, a black silk blouse and black heels, she grabbed her computer case and headed out the door. On the way to work, she picked up a large skinny vanilla latte with an extra shot of espresso, and made it to her office with minutes to spare, even after stopping to say a quick hello to Holly.

She'd just sat down and turned on her computer when she glanced up and saw Aiden heading toward her office, looking as gorgeous as ever in a charcoal-gray suit that fit his broad shoulders and lean frame to perfection. Memories of their time together, the intimate ones where they'd both been stripped bare, emotionally and physically, swamped her. There was no doubt that her feelings for this man had changed drastically during their time on the island, but she still had no idea where she stood with him, and she had to admit, it was a very vulnerable place to be.

His stride was purposeful, his body language tense, but it was the dark, angry look on his face that took her completely off guard. He entered her office, bringing with him a wave of foreboding that sent a chill up her spine…even though she didn't know *why*.

"Hi," she said, and smiled at him, trying to act normal, as if their time on the island hadn't changed anything between them when it came to working together. After all, that had been their promise—that what happened at the resort, stayed at the resort.

He didn't return her greeting, or her smile. Instead, he braced his hands on the opposite side of her desk and leaned toward her, his expression furious. "Are you seriously going to sit there and act as though you didn't screw me over?"

She jerked back, stunned by the bitterness dripping from his voice and the contempt in his gaze—as well as his abrasive, confusing question. "Excuse me?"

"Don't play stupid with me," he said, his voice a low, savage snarl. "You know exactly what I'm talking about. According to Perry, you pitched my goddamned matchmaking concept and won the St. Raphael account."

Two things hit Chloe at once—the startling fact that Aiden already knew about her meeting with Edward Luca, and that Luca had already chosen Aiden's campaign. On the heels of that knowledge came the more painful realization that Aiden had jumped to the automatic conclusion that she'd passed off his presentation as her own to *steal* the account from him.

A crushing pressure banded around her chest. She was devastated that he could so easily think the worst of her, that he honestly believed she'd betrayed him without giving her any opportunity to explain or defend herself against his harsh accusation.

A muscle in his jaw clenched, and his gaze narrowed. "Don't you have anything to say for yourself?"

She pushed aside the pain enveloping her heart, and let her own anger surface. "Why should I?" she said with a shrug that seemed to piss him off even more, but she didn't care. "You think you have it all figured out."

He opened his mouth to say something, but a brusque knock on her office door, and the sound of Perry's voice, stopped him before he could reply.

"Hey, you two," Perry said in a cheerful tone, oblivious to the heated conversation he'd just interrupted. "I need to see both of you in my office right away."

Perry moved on, and Aiden glared at her. "I guess we'll settle this in Perry's office." He pushed off her desk and stalked down the hallway toward the executive rooms.

Chloe slowly stood up, realizing her legs were shaking as she followed Aiden from a distance. The emotions swirling through her ranged from devastation and hurt to indignation. But it was the latter that she focused on as she took a seat beside Aiden in Perry's office.

Their boss looked from Aiden, to her, and frowned, finally sensing the animosity radiating off of Aiden. "Everything okay between you two?"

"No," Aiden said immediately. "Just to be clear, the matchmaking concept that Luca wants for his campaign was *my* idea, not Chloe's."

Perry looked taken aback by Aiden's very pointed claim. "When I called you last night, I never said it was Chloe's idea," Perry said carefully. "What I said was that Chloe pitched a matchmaking concept, Luca loved the idea, and is going with it."

Aiden still didn't look convinced, and it killed Chloe that he thought she was capable of doing something so deceitful, that after two years of working with her and spending a very intimate week together, he didn't trust her to have his back. The conversation they'd had about his ex-wife came back to her, how the one woman who should have been the most loyal to Aiden had betrayed him and their marriage for the sake of career.

She understood that he'd been burned badly in the past, but the fact that Aiden had lumped her into the same category as his ex-wife wrecked her in ways that made her wonder if she'd ever recover. Chloe was the first to admit that she was competitive when it came to her job, but she wasn't devious, underhanded or unscrupulous. She'd certainly never steal a concept or idea from a coworker to win an account.

Somehow, she managed to keep her own temper

in check and addressed Perry. "I'd like to explain exactly what happened yesterday."

Perry waved a hand in the air. "By all means, please do," he said, obviously anxious to clear up the misunderstanding.

"Yesterday, I overheard the boys with the Metro Ad Agency, who were being very persistent about pitching to Luca before they left the island, even though Edward told them he had meetings with both agencies this week," Chloe said, her tone calm and professional, despite the upheaval going on inside her. "Darryl assured him that their presentation was all Edward would need to see to make a final decision, so Luca gave them a meeting time. I decided to show up, too, because I wasn't about to let another agency pull one over on us."

The corner of Perry's mouth quirked up in a smile, as if he admired her gumption as much as Edward had.

"I had Aiden's flash drive with his presentation on it, because he'd shown me his campaign the day before and I forgot to give the drive back to him. But thank God I had it because I was not only able to pitch my own concept, but Aiden's, too, *separately,*" she added, making sure that Aiden understood she'd presented his campaign with just as much dedication as her own.

Finally, she glanced at Aiden. She should have been gratified by the stunned look on his too handsome face as he realized what she'd done *for* him, but the moment lacked any enjoyment because her heart just felt utterly broken.

"And it appears I did a damned good job on your behalf, since obviously Luca liked your idea the best. *You* and your concept won the account, not me," she said, her tone cool. "Congratulations."

"Chloe—"

She'd never know what Aiden had been about to say as she stood up, refusing to acknowledge him.

"What's going on with you two?" Perry asked.

Clearly, their boss suspected something had happened between them on the island. But what did any of that matter when she and Aiden were now adversaries? She'd not only lost Aiden as her lover, but as her friend. And that only compounded her devastation.

"If you'll excuse me, I'd like to get back to my office," she said, and walked out before her forced calm gave way to the full-blown anger still simmering inside her and she gave Aiden a real piece of her mind.

She strode into her office and sat down at her desk, watching as Aiden passed her office on the way to his. She tried to concentrate on answering the emails she'd gotten during her absence, but her mind wouldn't let her focus—on work, anyway—and she knew there was something she had to do to begin to put this whole mess with Aiden behind her. She wasn't sure if that was even possible, but she had to try. The hurt and resentment swirling inside her was only going to grow and get worse if she didn't confront Aiden and get everything out in the open between them.

With determination and a whole lot of irritation driving her, she headed over to Aiden's office and closed the door, because this was something she didn't want the entire floor overhearing. Aiden glanced up, his features etched with misery and contrition. But for her it was too little, too late.

"Chloe—"

She heard the apologetic note to his voice, and refused to let it soften or waylay her. "No, you don't get to talk," she said, quickly cutting him off. "You had your chance and you chose to be an ass and make all kinds of wrong assumptions. Now it's my turn to get a few things off my chest."

He sat back in his chair, quiet and wary.

She braced her hands on the opposite side of his desk, just as he'd done in her office earlier. "I could have just pitched my own concept and never mentioned yours, but I don't operate that way. We've always worked together, as partners, sharing ideas and concepts, and trusting one another. I've always been honest and real with you, and I've given you absolutely no reason to think I'd *ever* betray you."

Emotion clogged her throat, making her realize that this conversation had just turned very personal. Now that the floodgates were open, she couldn't stop the flow of words, or the overwhelming hurt she felt. "*You* left the island, Aiden. You left *me.* Without any kind of explanation. Like what we shared didn't matter to you at all. Not just the sex, but the intimate conversations we had, the way I trusted you with things that had happened in my past. You made me care again when I swore I didn't have it in me, and even worse, I fell in love with you."

The declaration tumbled out, and his eyes widened in shock, then clouded with regret, though he didn't respond—and she didn't want him to, anyway.

"It doesn't matter, though, does it?" she said, hating the pain and sadness in her voice. "Because when it comes right down to it, you don't trust me. You think I'm so focused on my career that I'd do whatever it takes to make it to the top, even steal an idea from my own colleague. From *you.* You want to believe that we're opposites and not compatible in any other way but in the bedroom, but you couldn't be more wrong. We have a lot in common, Aiden, if you'd just seen past the scars that your ex-wife left you with, instead of dwelling on them. I love my job, but I'd never be so underhanded. And just for the record, I'd never sacrifice a baby for the sake of my career. I'm the kind of woman who believes she can have a marriage, family and a profession, so do *not* lump me into the same category as your ex."

He shifted in his seat, his gaze darkening with anguish, and she knew her words had struck a very sore spot for him. Tears choked her, and before the moisture could fill her eyes and she completely lost her composure she turned around and left his office.

She heard him curse, but he didn't come after

her, and honestly, she was glad because she was so close to falling apart. Back in her office, she picked up her phone and dialed Perry's extension. Her call went to his voice mail, and she took advantage of that fact and left him a message, telling him she was exhausted and taking a few days off and would be in touch. With Aiden winning the St. Raphael account, it wasn't as though she was needed at the office.

All she wanted was to be alone with her misery. She needed time and space to figure out what her next move was going to be, because one thing was certain. She could no longer work with Aiden, because seeing him day after day, loving him the way she did, would absolutely destroy her.

She'd have to resign from the firm, she realized, as she tossed a few things into her briefcase so she could work from home. She had a great résumé and it wasn't as though it was the first time she'd started over with a new company. But she knew better than to make a rash decision in the heat of anger, not that she expected to change her mind—or calm down anytime soon.

She stilled when she caught sight of the piece of paper and the tagline for the resort she'd come up with on the spur of the moment and had written down after her presentation with Edward Luca, so she wouldn't forget it.

As if she ever could.

Find Love in Paradise. The laugh that escaped

Chloe held no humor at all. She might have found love in paradise, but her current reality was a nightmare.

AIDEN MET HIS brother Sam's inquisitive gaze from across the table at McGann's Pub, swallowed his pride, and confessed just how badly he'd botched things with the one woman who meant more to him than he ever could have imagined. "I screwed up with Chloe. Big-time." And the worst of it was, he didn't know if he'd be able to repair the damage he'd done.

He'd just finished telling Sam about what had happened between him and Chloe at the resort—from their agreed upon affair, to falling for her, to how he'd thought the worst of Chloe and her intentions when it came to pitching his campaign to Luca. He'd been miserable all day, wanting to apologize and make things right, but considering she'd taken the next few days off of work, Aiden knew she had nothing left to say to him, and no doubt wouldn't listen to him, either. She'd made that abundantly clear in his office that morning.

Not that he could blame her for blasting him with her indignation, which he fully deserved. His behavior, and the conclusions he'd jumped to, were inexcusable, even if they'd been a knee-jerk reaction based on his past. In reality, that made his assumption even worse, because Chloe was nothing like Paige when it came to honesty, integrity and her sense of loyalty. Those were characteristics that mattered to him, and over the past two years of working with Chloe, she'd proved time and again that she was a woman who lived by those traits.

She was right in telling him that she hadn't had to pitch his presentation to Luca, that she could have just promoted her own campaign and not even mention his. Yet she'd delivered his concept with enough persuasion to sell his idea to the vice president of the resort. She was the type of woman he'd always be able to trust to have his back, and he was sick to his stomach to think that he'd destroyed something so precious and rare.

Sam leaned forward in his seat, arms braced on the table and a cold bottle of Guinness in his hand. "Well, the first step to making amends with Chloe is admitting that you're wrong," Sam offered with a hint of humor, trying to make light of a dark situation. "And as difficult as I know that is for you to do, you just confessed that you screwed up."

Aiden raised a brow at his brother, not all that impressed with his worldly advice, but curious to hear what he'd suggest next. "And the second step?"

"Groveling. Lots of it." Sam grinned, as if he'd done his share and was an expert. "Women love that shit."

Aiden shook his head. "That might work with your playmates, but I don't think groveling is going to cut it with Chloe."

"Then just take the direct approach and man up,"

Sam said simply. "You owe her an apology and it's up to you to make her listen to it."

"Kind of hard to do when she won't even listen to me."

"You hurt her, so of course she's going to be standoffish and defensive." Sam took a drink of his beer, paused for a moment, then slanted him a curious look. "Do you care about Chloe?"

"Of course I do," Aiden said, his tone adamant.

"Do you want a *real* relationship with her?"

His brother's question brought up yet another huge obstacle standing in his way. "Yes. But even if Chloe forgives me, having any kind of real, open relationship with her is a whole other complication."

Sam frowned. "How so?"

Aiden swirled the amber liquid in his own bottle of beer. "Everyone at the agency is required to sign a strict no dating policy." It was a common practice in most high-profile firms, because of potential legal issues, conflict of interest and distractions at work. "An office relationship is grounds for termination of employment."

"Awww, shit," Sam muttered, sympathizing with Aiden's dilemma. "That sucks."

The rule definitely put Aiden at a disadvantage, because even if Chloe forgave him and wanted an open relationship, he wasn't willing to risk Chloe losing *her* job. He'd always planned to leave the firm to start up his own ad agency, was nearly there financially thanks to the bonus he'd gotten winning the

St. Raphael account, but this was Chloe's career, and she didn't deserve to be terminated. It was a catch-22 situation, and Aiden needed to figure out a way to not only get Chloe back, but keep their employment intact.

"Do you love her?"

Sam's quiet question made Aiden's heart beat faster. No matter how complicated, there was no denying that he did love Chloe. On the island, during their last night together, he'd known that she was the one he wanted to spend his life with, but he'd been so damned afraid to embrace the emotion and believe he could have a future with her. And then everything had unraveled from there, and he'd let those fears overrule rational thought.

A huge mistake he wanted to rectify.

"Yeah, I love her," he said gruffly.

Sam grinned. "Then do whatever it takes to make it happen, bro. Personally and professionally. I like Chloe and I think she's good for you. You two seem very compatible."

Aiden groaned at his brother's choice of word, since he and Chloe had just spent the past week debating the different aspects of compatibility. They'd each filled out a questionnaire that had deemed them opposites, yet a traditional matchmaker and her mystical flower had determined that they were soul mates. He could believe the results of those quizzes they'd taken, or he could take a chance on what Chloe made him feel. How he loved being with her, laughing with her, having deep, intimate discussions with her that bonded them emotionally.

Ironically, he chose to believe Hattie.

Chloe loved him, and knowing how she truly felt gave Aiden the hope that he still had a chance with her, to make things right and to let her know he wanted a future, and everything that came with it, with her.

Now he just had to figure out a way to have Chloe in his life, without jeopardizing her job.

12

Aiden spent most of the night tossing and turning, but by the time he arrived at work the following morning, he'd come up with a possible solution to his situation. It was a risky proposition, and it all depended on how lenient Perry was willing to be with Aiden's suggestion, but if his boss didn't agree, Aiden was ready and willing to walk out the door before he'd ever allow Chloe to lose her job.

Aiden was just reaching for the phone on his desk to call and request a meeting with Perry, when his intercom buzzed and Perry's personal secretary, Lena, spoke first. "Aiden, Mr. Perry would like to see you in his office immediately."

Lena rarely used the word *immediately,* which put an urgent spin to the request. Whatever was on Perry's mind, the other man wanted to address it post-haste, and that could either mean good news, or bad.

Aiden was prepared for either.

"I'll be right there," he said, and within a few minutes he was sitting across from Perry, who appeared calm, composed and very unreadable. Aiden had no idea what to expect.

Perry leaned forward in his chair and clasped his hands together on his desk, all business. "I just got off the phone with Edward Luca, and there's been a change in the campaign and what he wants."

"Okay," Aiden said hesitantly, wondering if Luca had instead decided on Chloe's flash mob concept, or worse, had elected to go with the Metro Ad Agency. A contract hadn't been signed, so the other man wasn't committed to any firm yet and could easily opt to go with a different idea or company.

"Now that he's had time to really think about your concept, and Chloe's, he's decided that he would like to incorporate elements of Chloe's presentation into the campaign, as well," Perry said, his expression remaining serious even though he was imparting some very exciting news. "It seems he likes the idea of using a flash mob as a viral marketing tool, with the focus being on the island matchmaker. He wants to mesh both concepts, and I agree that it could be a very effective campaign."

"That's fantastic," Aiden said, meaning it.

"I'm honestly glad you feel that way, because I wasn't sure you'd be okay sharing the account with Chloe. It would mean splitting the bonus with her, and working closely together for the next few months," Perry said pointedly. "And after what happened in my office yesterday between the two of you,

I have to wonder if that's going to be possible. Care to tell me what, exactly, happened on the island between yourself and Chloe?"

Perry's direct gaze met Aiden's, waiting for him to answer the question. Perry wasn't a stupid man, and probably had a good idea what had transpired on the island. Not just the misunderstanding of her pitching his presentation, but on a more personal level. And Aiden wasn't going to lie about it. This is where he intended to fight for Chloe, and prayed that it all worked out in the end.

He exhaled a deep breath. "Chloe and I broke the no dating policy," he admitted, trying to be as diplomatic as possible with his reply. "And I plan to continue seeing her outside of the office, if she'll accept my apology after yesterday's misunderstanding."

Perry's brows furrowed into a deep frown. "I figured something like that happened between you two, and now we have a situation where the tension has the potential to affect and hurt each of your efforts on the campaign." Perry's lips pursed, and anger flashed in his gaze. "This is exactly why the no dating policy exists. You do understand that this is grounds for termination, don't you? Not just for you, but Chloe, as well? I'm now in the position where I have to fire two of my best executives."

Aiden knew there was a firm stance on the no dating rule, because an intimate relationship with a colleague did tend to affect their working relationship. He'd seen it happen before, in other firms and even this office, and knew that there would be no exception for him and Chloe. One of them would have to leave, and Aiden planned for that person to be him.

"I have a compromise I'd like to offer," he said, because he cared for Chloe, loved her and wanted every aspect of a relationship with her to work. And that meant securing what was so important to her—her job and career. "I'm offering up my resignation, effective in three months, when the campaign for the St. Raphael account has been finalized. At that point, I'd like the entire account to become Chloe's, and *I'll* leave the firm."

Perry stared at him in shock. "You'd sacrifice your job for Chloe's, just like that?"

Aiden nodded, knowing he'd sacrifice a helluva lot more for the woman he'd fallen in love with and wanted in his life—every single day. "That's how much she means to me."

Perry considered his proposition for a moment, then spoke. "I think we could make that work."

Relief poured through Aiden, and he stood, feeling triumphant. "I'd like to get the agreement in writing, sir."

"Fair enough."

Perry stood and the two of them shook hands. "I have to say, I hate like hell losing you, but I have no doubt you'll be just fine."

"I know I will be," Aiden said with certainty. He might be starting his own firm sooner than he'd anticipated, but his decision felt good and right. And with Chloe by his side, supporting him, he knew he'd succeed.

Now, he just had to go and get the girl.

AFTER WORK, Aiden drove directly to Chloe's apartment, admittedly nervous about how this evening might end. He'd like to believe she'd forgive him, but the possibility existed that she wouldn't want to have anything to do with him or his apology.

He refused to even consider the latter.

He knocked on her door and heard footsteps nearing on the other side, then they stopped. Silence ensued. He knew she was looking through the peephole, and enough time passed that he was fairly certain she was going to completely ignore him.

"Open the door, Chloe," he said gently. "I need to talk to you."

No reply. He blew out a frustrated stream of breath and dragged his fingers through his hair. The stubborn woman was going to make him suffer—rightly so—but he could be just as determined.

"There's a lot I have to say, and I'm not going anywhere until I do," he persisted. "If I have to say it from this side of the door, I will, but I'd rather not have your neighbors listening in to the conversation."

Finally, the lock turned and the door opened, with Chloe standing on the other side. She wore a pair of sweatpants and a tank top. She wore no makeup and her hair was in a ponytail. He thought she was the most beautiful woman he'd ever seen—except for the irritable scowl on her face.

"Can I come in?" he asked.

Still not saying a word—though the apprehension in her body language spoke volumes—she stepped aside and let him enter. He'd never been inside her apartment before, and the living area was decorated in deep purples and forest-green. The room was warm, vibrant and inviting—like the woman herself when she wasn't so angry with him.

He turned to face Chloe, who was standing too far away for his liking, but he understood why the distance was there. He'd put it between them, and he hated himself for doing so.

She continued to stare at him, silent, not making any of this easy on him. "I owe you an apology for ever doubting that you'd do anything to hurt me," he said, the words heartfelt.

Her chin lifted an imperious inch. "Yes, you do."

She still wasn't softening, wasn't falling into his arms like he'd imagined. His gut tightened, but he hadn't thought it would be that easy. "I was an idiot, and I'm so sorry, Chloe. For ever believing that you are anything less than someone I can trust unconditionally. I'm sorry for leaving you alone on the island, instead of staying and talking things through with you."

She folded her arms over her chest. "Okay."

Okay? That's all he got…just *okay?*

Her tone was flat and emotionless, and it scared

the hell out of Aiden, made him fear that he was too late to repair any damage he'd done. He swallowed back the huge knot of uncertainty lodged in his throat and tried again. "Will you forgive me?"

"Why should I?" she said with a shrug of her shoulder.

He groaned. She was killing him with her cool indifference, and Aiden was forced to admit that his brother was right. He was going to have to grovel. Pull out the big guns to shake a real, emotional response from her.

"Why should you forgive me?" he asked, slowly stepping toward her. "Because I love you."

She gasped and took a step back, her eyes widening in shock.

Satisfied that he now had her full attention, he continued to move closer. "I'm so sorry that I let my past affect things between the two of us, because you are *nothing* like Paige. I was an idiot, and it wasn't until I'd lost you that I fully realized what holding on to the hurt from that betrayal was costing me. A future with you."

He stopped in front of her. "I know for a fact that you love me," he said, his gaze holding hers as he continued to list all the reasons why she *had* to accept his apology. "Because I want to be with you. Because I want to marry you and create a family together."

She shook her head furiously. "You can't just

come in here and say those kind of things to me, Aiden. Not unless you absolutely mean every word."

God, he loved her fire, her spirit. "I do mean every single word." He took her shaking hands in his, holding them tight. "There's always been something between the two of us. For two years we've worked together and denied our attraction, but a strong friendship developed. And then, on the island, being with you and seeing who you really are away from the office, well, it wasn't hard to fall in love with you. Even Hattie knew before I did," he said with a crooked smile. "I resisted, because of what happened with Paige, but there is no doubt in my mind that I love you, that I want to do whatever it takes to make it work between us."

"Oh, Aiden—" Her voice cracked with emotion, cutting off her words, and moisture shimmered in her eyes.

He panicked, his heart jolting in his chest. "Please tell me that those are tears of happiness."

"They are," she said, and laughed. "Oh, God, they are."

She wrapped her arms around his neck and kissed him, and the emotions that poured through Aiden were stronger than anything he'd ever felt before. He wholeheartedly embraced the feelings, and welcomed the need and desire she evoked in him.

The kiss deepened, the heat and passion between them escalating. Her moan of surrender was his undoing, making him desperate to be inside of her again, to feel that connection, and by mutual agreement they made their way to her bedroom. She was just as frantic as they tugged and pulled their clothes off, until they were both naked and he pressed her down onto the soft mattress. Framing her beautiful face in his hands, he lowered his head and took her mouth the same way he took her body…slowly, deeply, sensuously, until they were both unable to do anything but give in to the inevitable pleasure they created together.

Completely spent and ridiculously happy, Chloe snuggled against Aiden's side and rested her head on his shoulder, feeling more content than she could ever remember. Forgiving Aiden was easy, because she understood why he'd jumped to the conclusions he had, even if it had been a painful experience for her to go through. And, he'd groveled with such conviction and sincerity, which had gone a long way in proving to her that he was a man who could admit when he was wrong.

She sighed and smiled to herself as he lazily stroked a warm hand along her hip and trailed his fingers along the dip of her waist. She was in love, Aiden loved her, and her world couldn't be more perfect…until she remembered the one thing that could tear them apart.

A surge of panic rippled through her, and she lifted her head and stared down at Aiden, who looked up at her with slumberous, sexy eyes. "What are we going to do about work?" she asked. "If anyone finds out that you and I are in a relationship..."

"Perry already knows. I told him about us."

"You did?" Aiden looked so calm and unconcerned, while Chloe couldn't stop the dread swirling in her stomach. "Are we both fired?" She wasn't giving up Aiden, but she would have rather quit the firm, rather than have a termination on her employment record.

"Nobody's fired, and you still have a job," he said, smiling at her. "In fact, Luca called Perry and wants to incorporate both our concepts for his campaign, and so I made a deal with Perry. I'm going to stay for the next three months to help you finalize the St. Raphael campaign, and then I'm resigning from the firm and the account becomes yours, along with half of the bonus."

Her jaw dropped open. "What? You can't do that!"

"I can and I did," he assured her. "It was either that, or one or both of us would be fired. I wasn't going to risk you losing your job."

She swallowed hard, realizing what he'd done for her, what he'd sacrificed. "But what about you?"

"I'm good. Honest." He lifted his hand and tenderly caressed her cheek. "I've been planning on starting up my own ad agency for a while now. This just pushes up the time frame a bit faster. And guess what?"

Humor danced in his eyes, making her smile and curious to know what amused him. "What?"

"If you ever want to come to work for me, which I'm hoping you will at some point in the future, you won't have to worry about a no dating policy." A sinful grin curved his lips. "In fact, I'll have to insist that you sleep with the boss."

She laughed, knowing she'd be taking advantage of that special perk. "You've got yourself a deal."

* * * * *

SPECIAL EXCERPT FROM

Karen Foley delivers a sexy new *Uniformly Hot!* story
Here's a sneak peek at

Free Fall

So you were, what, just a teenager when you left?" Jack asked.

Maggie tipped her chin up and looked directly at him. "I was lmost nineteen. Old enough to be married."

He blanched. "Were you? Married?"

If he was going to be living around here, he would eventually earn the truth. Ten years wasn't nearly enough time for the ocals to have forgotten. But there was no way she was going o fill him in on the sordid details. She'd endured enough umiliation at being jilted; the last thing she wanted was this nan's pity.

"I came close," she finally said. "But we didn't go through vith it."

"So you ran, and you didn't look back."

Maggie looked sharply at him, startled by his astuteness. 'My leaving had nothing to do with that," she fibbed. "I simply lecided to pursue my dream of becoming a photographer."

"So what about now? Is there someone waiting for you back n Chicago?"

She shook her head. "No. There's nobody like that in Chicago."

"Good."

And just like that, the air between them thrummed with

HBEXP79761

energy. Jack took a step toward her, and Maggie held h breath. There was something in his expression—somethin hot and full of promise—that made her heart thump heavil against her ribs, and heat slide beneath her skin. She couldn remember the last time a man had made her feel so aware herself as a woman. Reaching out, he traced a finger along he cheek.

“It’s getting late. You should go to bed.” His voice was lo and Maggie thought it sounded strained.

Erotic images of the two of them, naked and entwined be neath her sheets, flashed through her mind.

In three weeks, she would return to Chicago, and the likeli hood of ever seeing Jack Callahan again was zero. Did she hav the guts to reach out and take what she wanted, knowing sh couldn’t keep it? She wasn’t sure, and suddenly she didn’t care.

Turning, she opened the back door to the house, and the looked at Jack. “Why don’t you join me?”